LABYRINTH

A small collection of fantastical short stories

J. David Hanlin, Jr.

This is an original work of fiction. Names, characters, places, and incidents either are the product of the author's imagination or are used fictitiously. Any resemblance to actual persons, living or dead, or actual events is entirely coincidental.

Cover design by J. David Hanlin, Jr.

Cover photography: Pamela Hanlin. Used by permission.

Back cover photography and design: J. David Hanlin, Jr.

ISBN 978-0-9979077-1-1

For my family

Contents

MegaBat

"In 2006, our country was invaded by an unseen yet powerful agent of such diabolical power, it held the potential to decimate millions of lives over the span of just a few short years. And now, it seems we have reached a frightening tipping point, as we prepare to helplessly witness a vital species of mammal evanesce into extinction."

That was how Dr. Samantha Strong's explanation was going to commence - or so she thought. It sounded good in her head, and looked great on paper, but that was before all hell broke loose in the lab where she had been lead researcher and scientist, located in upstate New York, just outside Albany, close to where the first outbreak of WNS, or White-Nose Syndrome, had been discovered in an exploratory cave dwelling of Northern Long-Eared Myotis…Bats. In an attempt to find a cure for WNS, a condition where a white fungus grows on the muzzles, wings and ears of stricken bats, and which also has mortality rates of over 90% among afflicted species and colonies, Dr. Strong, in a radical and desperate move, developed a steroidal anti-fungal agent that was 100% effective in eradicating the disease in test subjects from her lab, but which turned out to also have a *huge* downside.

Composing a scientific memorandum seemed necessary to her right now, perhaps maybe pointless, as well, but she felt that an explanation of some kind had to be put on record. As she sat at her desk, in her home office, she stared blankly at the paragraph she had just written. Her laptop screen was the only source of illumination in the room, and as its light reflected off of her stressed eyes, her thoughts faded from what the next sentence would be, and she began to think back on how all of this had come to be: the discovery of WNS, the rapid spread of the fungus across the northern states and down south as far as Kentucky and Virginia, the estimates of millions of bats dying over the past seven years, and the desperation over a variety of government agencies, councils and panels, all trying to work in unison to come up with a cure that would end the decimation of entire species of bat, as extinction coldly stared many of the mammals in the face.

Sam's job, as head of the scientific team assigned to search for a cure, was to thoroughly study the disease itself, conduct extensive biological and chemical testing on exposed test subjects from six species of bat - the little brown bat, Indian Bat, Northern Long-Eared, Virginia big-eared bat, gray bat, and two afflicted vampire bats from the Buffalo Zoo - and come up with at least one viable solution to combat the fungus, which was named *Pseudogymnoascus destructus*, and to find said solution in an expedited manner. The timeline she and her team were given was a year or less, which was a ludicrous goal, especially by scientific standards, but to say "time is of the essence" here was an understatement. Not only were bat populations being decimated at an extreme rate, but the agricultural and economical effects their losses were having added up to millions, if not billions of dollars, due to crop devastation and insect infestation, while the loss of pollination and seed dispersal that bats provide the environment itself was practically unquantifiable.

Sam and her team – two fellow colleagues, plus two zoology interns from the University of Albany – had actually found a breakthrough when they created an anti-fungal injection called *Myobetachloradone*, aka serum-187, which they dubbed mBCD, for short. The administration of mBCD had a positive effect on the fungus, but initial doses weren't potent enough to come close to eradicating the disease from any of the test subjects. So, in a radical act of desperation and time-saving, she had the idea to lace the injections with a homemade cocktail of steroid plus a customized protein compound Sam called MGH, or mylo-growth hormone. The main reason for the addition of the cocktail was to assist the bats in recovering from the emaciated state that WNS leaves its victims in, which is the main cause of mortality in the first place. Sam was afraid the cocktail might be too potent, so she instructed her team to give increases in dosage in micrograms, being careful not to give too much too soon, knowing the fragile state of health the bats were in.

Then, in a curious occurrence of irony, the week that the mBCD/MGH injections were given, half of Dr. Strong's team, as well as herself, came down with the flu, which apparently had descended down on the Albany community like a mini-plague. She held out as long as she could in the lab, but finally relented to her symptoms and took a day off to recover, while leaving instructions with one of the lab interns, Floyd Hardwick, to increase dosages for the bats by .10 mcg each. However, Floyd mistakenly read the dosages to be 10 mg increases, and each bat inadvertently received the wrong amounts. To the team's shock and surprise, not only was the mistake non-lethal to the subjects, but each bat had a complete eradication of the disease within 24 hours of administration. The group, sick or not, gathered quickly in the lab to celebrate in cautious jubilee; Dr. Strong, as elated as she was, hesitated to alert the various government departments immediately, knowing that complete eradication had to be confirmed, and other follow-up tests had to be conducted over the next few days, in order to draw accurate, necessary conclusions to their findings. But the results were extremely encouraging, nonetheless!

On the second day after the MGH administration, all test subjects began to show both weight increase and some body mass growth. In fact, there was extreme body growth. Each bat grew at such a rapid rate, that they quickly became too large for their lab cages, and the team had to bring in larger enclosures. While this was happening, Dr. Strong, who had not left the lab since the breakthrough, was monitoring each bat's vital signs, behavior, etc, and noticed that half of them, as their growth spurt progressed, developed first tachycardia, then at 48 hours post-admin, all six had died of cardiac arrest. The species of gray, VA long-eared, and Indian bats lacked the cardiovascular system strong enough to keep up with the demands that the enhanced serum-187 had placed on them. That left the not-so-little brown bats, the Northern Myotis, and the vampire bats…and Sam made sure to keep a watchful eye on all of them, especially the vampires. She and the team took notice to behavioral changes that were also occurring in the subjects, which had been subtle at first, but as time went on, after the 48 hour mark and especially after the other bats died, the remaining ones began to show increased aggression, as well as appetites, on top of size growth. These increases were accelerating at such a rate that Dr. Strong was afraid they would quickly reach an unmanageable state, and she began to fear what kind of mortal danger everyone would be in if the bats reached the sizes of large dogs, or even that of jungle cats…the kind that enjoyed the taste of meat. Comparisons like that were unprecedented, and every decision made now was a guessing game; she knew all actions had to err on the side of caution – it was a matter of *their* own life and death, she felt.

Everyone was tired, and some lab personnel were still sick, so Sam decided to send them all home that night. She knew the entire team would have to be well rested and prepared for whatever the next few days had in store for them. Before leaving, they were able to successfully tranquilize the bats, assuring little to no activity during the night, and the last person didn't leave the lab until the final subject was put under. The group quietly walked to their cars in the adjacent parking garage, knowing they would have to return after only eight hours or so, but any rest was welcome, and all of them slept like babies; she always thought that when it came to sleep, quality always surpassed quantity (for the most part). Unfortunately, when the group returned to the lab early the next morning, their worst fears had been realized.

To the group's horror, the bats had grown exponentially overnight; they were humungous now. Their aggressive natures led them to attempt to chew and bite at the bars on their cages, like rabid beasts desperate for freedom. They were at least 20 times their normal size, and Dr. Strong knew something had to be done to stop all of this, with haste.

The sense of panic was palpable in the lab, and Sam didn't hesitate to act on her instincts, as she exclaimed to her coworkers, "Put the subjects down; put them all down, now! We have to stop this, immediately. They're growing too fast- soon we won't be able to control them, let alone move them into larger containments. Shoot each one with Tributone; that should put them down for good." Even thought it was difficult to do with all of the violent activity occurring in the cages, they were successful at administering the lethal cocktail to the brown bat and one of the vampires (the smaller of the two), but while the group was occupied with those two bats, both the myotis and second vampire bat violently broke out of their respective enclosures, and immediately began attacking each other. The vampire bat had a distinct size advantage, resembling a dark flying smart car at this point, while the myotis, with its huge ears that had to be over three feet tall, was about half the size of its opponent. The vampire bat used its wings to push the other into a corner of the lab, and preceded to repeatedly beat the head of the myotis with its huge appendages, and when the smaller foe seemed to stop struggling to escape, stunned by the concussive blows, the vampire bat lunged at it, sinking its razor-sharp teeth into its skull and staying there as the myotis bled out, spurting dark blood into the air and all over the lab's wall and floor. The scientists watched in stunned silence from across the room, frozen in fear. After a brief minute, the giant predator turned its head from its victim and over toward the awed group, shrieking at the top of its lungs and spewing blood out from its crimson toned mouth, which was when Sam screamed to everyone, "Out of the lab, now!"

She was closest to the door, and opened it quickly and pushed her colleague, Dr. Eileen Bowen, into the Observation Room that was adjacent to the lab, as the rest of them followed behind. Floyd Hardwick and the second intern, Cassie Morland, were the last to approach the exit. She got out first, but just before Floyd reached the door, the bat leapt onto his back from behind, and sunk its teeth into the young man's left shoulder. Sam had been holding the door for everyone, and all she could do was quickly slam it shut and lock it, walk slowly into the OR, and helplessly watch through the window as the bat tore the man's upper torso apart, his white lab coat now soaked in dark liquid and his high pitched screaming now suppressed by the walls that separated the room from the lab. The group was frightened and in shock, and slowly made their way to the exit doors on the opposite side of the room, still staring through the large glass window into the lab, watching the bat's body rise and fall over its victim. Another scientist, Dr. Albert Canterra, muttered out loud, "My God, that poor boy. He had a wife and little girl...how could this happen? This isn't possible, is it?" Dr. Bowen yelled back at him as she reached for the exit door, "Of course it's possible, you're seeing it with your own eyes, aren't you?! We need to get the hell out of here!" With that, she flung herself at the door and it swung open with a loud noise that echoed throughout the room, and the bat took notice of the sound, stopping its rampage and then looked through the observation window, into the room and at the occupants. It shrieked again, spraying blood all over the glass, and began thrusting its head and body against the window. The door between the rooms was magnetically locked, but the large observation window was completely vulnerable to an animal of this size and ferocity, and with every successive strike of the bat's head, the window would crack. Dr. Strong gathered her thoughts, and then said the obvious: "We all have to evacuate the building and find safety outside of these walls. Get to your vehicles as fast as you can, drive to your homes…and then just pray." She knew she had to notify the Forestry Dept. and the authorities, but a 9-1-1 call would have to wait until she found shelter for herself. There was no cell reception in the building, and there was no time to make a call using a landline inside the OR, so it would have to wait a few more minutes until she was at least in the parking lot. As they made for the exit, the bat, which had been relentless at striking the window, finally hit the glass with such force that the entire pane shattered into thousands of pieces, and the bat flew clumsily into the room, throwing chards of glass and furniture in all directions. Sam, glancing back one last time as she made her way to the door, could see the creature's head was fully covered in either the student's or its own blood, or probably both, and as it lifted its bloodied head to the ceiling and shrieked in her direction, she closed the exit door. "Look out!" Dr. Canterra yelled at her, as he and Cassie moved a vending machine onto its side and pushed it in front of the door. "This might buy us some precious seconds, Sam." She wasn't going to argue with him, and the three of them ran furiously straight down the hallway, which lead to two more doors that poured them out directly onto the upper level of the building's parking structure.

As they burst out into the parking lot, they heard the OR's doors crash open, and turned back to see the vending machine sliding down the hallway, and the bat, whose wings were too large to extend out and allow flight down the corridor, stumbled its way towards them. The group spread out in all directions, with Dr. Canterra hustling off to the right and down the stairs to a lower level. Sam's car was just to her left, sitting next to one of the lab's white cargo vans, and she sprinted over to it, but tripped halfway there, falling onto the cement garage surface, landing on her right knee and scraping it up badly. As blood streamed down her shin, Sam made her way to the car, then suddenly realized that her keys were not in her lab coat pocket, but she had put them in her purse, which was left in her desk drawer back in the OR. Panicked, she looked over to the closed doors of the building, just as the bat crashed through them, and she ducked down out of sight, behind her vehicle-a Miata. This did not give her a decent hiding place, she felt, and she decided to crawl around the front of the car, over to the lab van, and hopefully find better cover using it. When she reached it, she painfully stood up, and cautiously peered through the van's windshield, where she could now see the bat's position by the doors. It stood there smelling the air and spreading its wings out to their farthest positions, almost as if it was stretching them before taking off. Sam took a step back with her left foot, but landed on loose gravel and her foot slipped back about six inches, making a scraping sound that the bat couldn't help but hear. She instinctively fell to the ground, and looked underneath the van, over to the bat, whose feet were on the ground one moment, then she saw them rise and disappear from view; it had flown upward, and she then flung herself under the vehicle, barely having enough room to fit. Sam was now lying on her back, with her face staring straight up at the van's transmission, and she turned her head to the side just as the bat, which had flown directly over to the van, landed on top of its roof, pushing the undercarriage down a few inches and barely missed the side of Sam's face. As it violently rocked the van back and forth, trying to figure out what happened to its prey, the bat flapped its wings torridly, causing a swell of dirt and dust to envelope the entire parking space, and Sam found herself having to hold her breath to stop from breathing in all of the contaminated air, which she knew would cause her to sneeze. That would be a bad thing, she felt, and was able to bring her left hand up to her face to cover her mouth and nose. More glass fell to the ground, and she closed her eyes as not to get hit by the smaller pieces that were in the dirt being flung all around her. Sam could feel her heart beating rapidly, knowing that she was in extreme mortal danger, now. With her eyes closed, she could only hear what the bat was doing, and the deafening sound of it crashing its feet and body onto the top of the van, along with the shattering of glass and various parts of the van's mechanical parts moving in unfamiliar ways, were enough to fill her mind with terror, and the noise seemed to last for a week. However, as she tried not to cry or panic as she lay there helplessly on her back, the noise of the van shaking stopped, as did the bat's shrieks and the sound of metal smashing and glass breaking. She slowly opened her eyes, finding herself looking out from under the van, toward the wall of the building, There was no wind from the flapping of wings, no shaking of the vehicle, and no noise echoing throughout the garage. She laid there for a moment, moving her hand away from her face, slowly taking deep, silent breaths. A minute passed, then another. Still, there was nothing happening. She waited another couple of moments, then cautiously slid herself over to the side of the van that was closest to her car, feeling her back getting cut up by all of the various remnants of the attack left on the pavement. Sam peered up at the ceiling of the structure, its lights still working and illuminating the parking spaces, and no sign of the bat around her.

She stood up between the car and the van, her knee throbbing in pain and covered in dried blood, now, and slowly limped toward the smashed doors of the building, and upon arriving there, before she walked inside to retrieve her purse and keys, she turned to look around the structure. It was deathly silent; all she could hear was the humming of the lights that lit up the entire third level. The bat must have realized that it had its freedom now, and flew off out the front opened end of the parking lot, up into the Albany night. She fought back tears of joy and relief, and reached into her lab coat pocket for her cell phone, so she could find the number for the Forestry Dept. and call them from the OR. First though, she had to find something to drink, or she was going to die of thirst.

THE GOBLIN IN THE GLEN

Patrick and his twin sister, Shannon, wondered up the small rise, along the dirt path that they had followed all the way from their backyard earlier that morning, and when they reached the top of the grassy hill, they could finally see the forest ahead. Its dark green colors were a stark contrast to the bright yellows and lighter shades of green of the fields and meadows that covered the surrounding land, as far as the eye could see, including all the way back in the direction of the children's home, where their parents were both very sick from a terrible illness that left them bed ridden and unable to leave the house. The siblings were tasked to accompany each other to these woods, called Densmoor Forest, to look for a plant called the trufungus weed, and bring a bushel of them back to the house. The weeds would be used as the main ingredient in a hot broth that would help their parents get better, and the only place the weeds were known to grow were in the forest that lay in front of them. The children, only twelve years of age, were the only ones who could make the half-day's journey to the forest, since their house and property were quite isolated from any other neighboring family's land. In fact, the forest was closer, in distance, to their house than the nearest neighbor's house was; and even if a neighbor did live closer, the trafungus weed wasn't something most households kept in their possession, simply because going into the forest to get some did not seem to be a popular journey that anyone wanted to take.

Before the brother and sister left that morning, their father, sick as he was, made sure he told them two things. First, get in and out of the forest as quickly as possible, because if they went into it and took too long looking for the weed, or if they lost track of time exploring inside the woods, it would get very dark as the afternoon fell into evening, and he feared they wouldn't be able to find their way out of the forest; it was a dangerous place to be at night, and he didn't want his kids to be lost, cold and frightened in that dark place by themselves. Secondly -and this was just as (if not more) important- he warned them of an old legend that said a creature guarded the forest…an old, surly goblin that acted as guardian of the woods from any strangers that came looking to enter the forest. Stories were told of the goblin tricking anyone going near the forest into completing strange and difficult tasks, in order to not only discourage the visitors from attempting to make their way past him and into the woods, but to also simply amuse himself as he watched the strangers struggle and toil with the perplexing challenges he gave them. If a task was denied or not completed, then the creature forbid entrance into "his forest" and sometimes was said to even get angry enough to put a curse on the unsuspecting travelers. There were stories told of men losing all of their teeth, and women having their hair fall out – even the hair on their eyes brows! The children were taken back a bit by all of this, and their father assured them that they were just stories and rumors, made up a long time ago in order to play on the mystery of Densmoor, since it was so far away and not much was known about it, in the first place. He told the kids that the point he was making was to not talk to any strangers along the way, and to stick to the job of arriving there, finding the weeds and promptly returning home before the sun went down. Because the sooner they were home, the sooner their mother and he could start to feel better.

After their father spoke to them, the twins set off for their daylong journey, right as the sun was coming up. It was a bright, sunny morning, and they expected it to be that way for the whole trip. Shannon's job was to carry the bag of tools that they would use to dig and pull the weeds from the ground, and Patrick was given a basket to carry. They made sandwiches that were put in the basket, along with some fruit and jars of water, with the plan to eat lunch when they arrived at the edge of the forest, then use the empty basket to carry the trufungus weeds in on their way back. Patrick was a little upset over his duty, telling his sister that boys carry tools and girls carry baskets. But Shannon countered that by saying that she was technically born first, thus the older of the two, which made her more responsible; hence, the oldest gets to carry the tools. This argument occurred in the house, before they left, and their mother heard them from her bedroom. "Your sister's right, Patrick! Do as Shannon says," she yelled to them, then coughed and sniffled a few times before falling back to sleep. Disappointed, Patrick accepted the task of basket carrier, and the two ate a quick breakfast of eggs and oatmeal, and then, with the rising sun to their backs, they walked through the backyard, past a rickety gate their father had made along time ago, that was connected to a small stone wall that surrounded their property. They walked past chickens, goats and their parent's horses, which were too large for either of them to ride. A dirt path began after they passed the gate, and lead straight off ahead, far away from the house, which was the way to the forest.

The path was pretty much a straight line (more or less), leading away from their house, surrounded on both sides by green and lush fields of tall grass that eventually blended in with large pastures and rolling hills, while also winding through a few thickets of trees and shrubbery. The sun moved across a blue, cloudless sky throughout the morning, but it wasn't a very hot day, the children noticed. Every now and then, a slight breeze would wisp by their heads, carrying with it the aromas of heather and jasmine, which Shannon enjoyed taking deep breaths of; Patrick didn't take notice, though. His attention was fixed on spotting animals running around, trying to find rabbits or foxes or squirrels. While he was looking down at the ground, Shannon watched the various birds that would fly overhead, picking out the different kinds by looking at the colors of their feathers: orange of Robins, red of Cardinals, blue of Blue Jays…she even saw a couple of doves, with their white feathers easy to spot against the blue sky.

After walking all morning, the children were now standing at the top of a small hill that rolled down a slight slope to the last bit of green field, before the darkness of Densmoor Forest began. From this height, they could see the tree line stretch all the way to the right and left, and it looked like a very, very large area to cover, now. They worried that finding the trafungus weed wouldn't be easy, and that it might take them longer to find it than they had thought. At this point, the siblings decided to walk down to the bottom of the hill and find a good place to enter the woods, but before doing so, they would first eat their lunch, and then venture into the forest.

The dirt path continued down the slope and toward the tree line ahead of them. The grass in the glen that they were heading into was as tall as they were, so much so that Patrick, walking a few steps ahead of his sister, didn't see the creek in front of him until he almost walked right into the water! Shannon came up beside him, and they were both surprised that neither of them had noticed the creek from on top of the hill, because it ran right across the glen, practically splitting it into two, running parallel to the forest on the other side. Shannon looked around and found a long stick, leaned over the water and dipped it down into the water, checking to see how deep it was. She was able to put almost half of it into the water before it hit the bottom, and they both felt that it was too deep to go into and cross, because who knows how deep in would be in the middle. The two began looking around for a different way to hopefully get over the creek, and when Shannon stood on her tippy toes and looked to her right, over the tall grass, she could see a stone bridge that led across the creek, and said "There's a bridge over there! We can use it to cross over!" Patrick smiled at the thought of not having to get his clothes wet, and he took his sister's hand as they hurried through the field to where the nearside of the bridge began. There was an open area of land just before the entrance, which would make for a great place to rest a bit and eat their lunch.

Shannon wondered why the path led straight to the creek, and not to the bridge, but she didn't let it bother her for more than a second. She was hungry and a bit tired of walking, so sitting down and having a bite to eat was exactly what she needed.

When they got to the bridge, she noticed the stones looked just like the ones that surrounded their house and yard, and stood only a couple of feet high, while the bridge itself was about ten feet across, wide enough to fit a wagon through, she thought. Shannon also saw something that immediately caught her eye: both sides of the bridge's entrance were cluttered with beautiful purple flowers that she had never seen before. She was so excited at the sight of these, that she let go of Patrick's hand and ran over to a patch of the flowers, pulled a handful out of the ground, put her nose to the petals and took a long, deep breath. The aroma was something she had never smelled before, and she wanted to take another breath of them, but before she could, she felt herself getting very sleepy. She felt her head get light, and her eyelids became heavy as she yawned deeply and felt her legs get weak, and the tool bag fell from her arms, down to the ground. Patrick saw what was happening, and he dropped the basket of food and caught her, just as she was about to collapse. He was then able to sit her gently on the ground, with her back against the stone wall. "Shannon!" he yelled. "Wake up, Shannon! We need to eat and get to the forest!" He reached out to her shoulders and shook her a little, hoping that would jar her awake, but it didn't help. She didn't respond to any of his pleas; she just sat there sleeping, with the same smile on her face that she had when she smelled the purple flowers.

Just then, as Patrick began to worry about what he was going to do if he couldn't wake Shannon up out of her untimely nap, he heard a strange voice that seemed to come from under the bridge. "Oh, dear. It seems the young girl has mistakenly taken a sniff of a very pretty flower, but one that has a nasty defensive reaction when pulled from its roots." Patrick, scared and surprised, jumped back and watched as a strange creature, with yellow and green skin, walked up from under the bridge and stood over Shannon. His skin helped him blend in with the surrounding grassy field, and his body was very skinny and very wrinkly. He wore no shirt, only torn up shorts that revealed long, boney legs, but Patrick thought his face was the strangest feature about him: he had a pointed chin, thin lips, barely a nose, big dark round eyes, stringy long black hair, and pointed ears, like small arrows were coming out of the side of his head.

"Who are you?" he asked the creature.

"Why, I am the goblin that lives in this glen, my boy. Surely you've heard of me?"

His voice sounded like something he could have dreamt of, Patrick thought. It didn't sound like an adult, nor did it sound like a child's voice, either; if an animal could talk, this is what it would sound like, he decided.

"No…well, yes, I have heard of you," Patrick answered. "From our father, who mentioned you to us this morning, before we left our house to come here."

"Your father…I see." The goblin paused for a moment, then he continued. "My intuition tells me that he sent you and your sister here, to look for something in the forest. Do you know what that is, 'intuition'?"

Patrick shook his head. "I've never heard that word before."

"It means being able to guess the facts or truth about something, my boy. So, am I?"

"Are you what?" Patrick asked.

"Am I right? About why you both are here, in my glen?"

Patrick hesitated, then answered, "We're here to find trufungus weeds, and bring them home with us. Our parents are both very sick, and need the weeds to help them get better."

"Ah, I see now." The goblin turned and looked to the woods, then turned back to Patrick, pointed at him and said, "You want to take things from my forest, do you? I'm not sure I can allow that, young man. Not unless you can give me something in return. Quid pro quo, if you will. Do you know what that means, 'quid pro quo'?"

"No, I don't." Patrick answered.

"It means, you do for me, and I in turn do for you. A favor for a favor, as it were. I'll let you go into Densmoor Forest to retrieve your weeds, but you'll need to do something for me, in return."

Patrick became confused. "What do you mean? What would I have to do for you?" He started to feel more nervous, at the thought of having something else to do on top of finding the weeds- by himself now-and also finding a way to wake his sister up when he was done.

The goblin stroked his long, pointy chin a few times, then answered, "There are quite a number of birds that live in the forest, among them is a family of robins. Now, I'm sure you have tasted eggs from a chicken before, cooked and eaten over a delicious morning breakfast with your family. Well, I assure you, the taste of a robin's egg is exponentially more delicious than any chicken's egg you've ever tasted, my lad. I have only enjoyed the meal of a robin's egg once before, and I do so desire to have one, again. So, that will be your task, to search out a robin's nest with a clutch of eggs in it, take one from the nest and bring it back to me, along with your precious trufungus weeds, and I shall consider our deal complete."

Patrick did not hesitate to ask the goblin, "What about my sister? Will I be able to wake her up when I get back?

The creature laughed at this question and answered, "Oh, of course, my son. After you bring back my robin's egg, I'll tell you how to awaken her from her slumber. It will be quite simple, I assure you.

Just return with the egg and weeds, and everything will be right as rain."

Patrick, looking at his sister, knew he had no choice but to say yes to the goblin's request.

He looked across the bridge at the dense thicket of trees in the forest, then up at the sun in the sky, knowing that it was well past midday, and his time was running out to get in and out of the woods before evening came around, when he and his sister would really be in trouble.

"Okay, I'll do it," he said to the goblin, who was now leaning against the side of the bridge, chewing on a long piece of grass.

"Excellent! Then I shall not keep you here any longer, my boy. Take what tools you need, and follow the path across the bridge. It will lead you directly into the heart of the forest. The trufungus weeds should be fairly easy to find, as they are ubiquitous throughout Densmoor. A robin's nest might prove more difficult to locate; my advice is to look for a robin flying over head, and then follow it back to its nest, wait for it to leave again, and climb up the tree, to the nest, grab an egg and climb back down. So very simple, even a child can do it." The goblin then thought to itself for a moment. "One final note: You may find that the forest has a mystical quality to it, and you may see or hear things that you normally wouldn't expect to, but that sometimes happens to strangers in Densmoor, so don't be alarmed or frightened, laddie."

The creature smiled and looked over at Patrick, who was going through the tool bag, taking out what he would need to bring with him, then he knelt down next to Shannon and whispered to her, "Don't worry, I'll be back as fast as I can, then you'll wake up and we'll be on our way home right after, I promise."

Patrick started walking across the bridge, when the goblin made one last comment.

"Remember, you must bring me one robin's egg. That is the deal."

"I know," he replied, then stopped and turned around and looked at the goblin. "You have to promise me you won't harm my sister while I'm gone."

"My boy, for a robin's egg, I will guard her with my life. You have my word."

Patrick had no choice but to trust him, so he turned back to the forest and continued crossing the bridge, landed on the dirt path on the other side of the creek, and followed it straight up to the edge of the tree line. As he approached, he could hear the sounds of the forest getting louder: the chirping of birds, and the various noises of crickets, locusts, and other insects that he couldn't see but he had heard before, around his house and farm. As he reached the edge of the forest, the sun fell behind the tall trees lining up in front of him, and the shade felt cool and brought an air of fear of the unknown to Patrick, but he knew he had to forge ahead on the path, and hope he could quickly find the "ubiquitous" weeds as the goblin put it, whatever that meant. Patrick hoped it was a good thing, and he took a deep breath as he briskly walked into Densmoor Forest, staying focused on the task at hand. What gave Patrick confidence was knowing what the trufungus weed looked like. It's a short plant, with five large green leaves growing out of its stem, resembling the lettuce leaves that grew in his parents' garden. However, the trufungus weed had a bright yellow trim that lined the outside of each leaf, which even in the dark shade of the dense forest, should be easy to distinguish between other plants and weeds on the ground.

As he walked into the woods, Patrick felt the air he was breathing feel heavy and warm, and he began to sweat from the warmth that the forest kept within itself. He looked up to the trees and branches as he walked, seeing many types of birds flying around. He noticed a cardinal, bright red against all of the brown and green colors of the trees and shrubbery, flying across the path, diving down to the ground, behind bushes to his left, then darting back up in the air, across to his right and disappearing among the thicket of branches overhead. Patrick then saw a squirrel climb down one of the trees that lined the dirt path, which was getting narrower now, and it hopped onto the ground and picked up an acorn it had found among the roots of the tree, and sat there eating it as Patrick walked by. No sooner did he look away from the squirrel that a mouse sprinted across the path in front of him, into the plants to his left, with a fox, orange with a black bushy tail, chasing right after him. They both were out of sight, but Patrick could hear the chase continue into the forest…and he secretly hoped the mouse would get away. The flurry of action and wildlife that surrounded him took his mind off of his task at hand, but after a couple of minutes, he focused again. He walked slowly forward, carefully scanning the ground on both sides of the path, and then his eyes landed on a spot just to his right, a few yards off of the path, where a large tree trunk sat, and surrounding it grew the green and yellow-lined leaves of the trufungus weed – he had found some!

He rushed over to the trunk, knelt down in the dirt next to the plants, and reached into the tool bag. He brought out a pair of gloves, a little shovel and clipping sheers. The gloves were his father's so they were large over his hands, but Patrick was still able to grip the shovel without them falling off. He began to dig around the roots of the weeds, then pulling the leaves with one hand, he took the sheers to the exposed roots and cut them, going as deep as he could, making sure he took as much of the plant as possible. The leaves weren't just important to get, but the roots were necessary, too, their father had told them. Patrick had found four large, healthy plants on this spot alone, and he carefully went around the tree trunk and removed each one and placed them all in the tool bag, which was large enough to carry more, but he and his sister were told only three or four plants were needed. So, he packed up the weeds, walked back to the path and began to look around for a robin to follow back to its nest.

The amount of activity that occurred over Patrick's head was dizzying. As he looked around for a robin, other birds constantly flew from tree to tree, branch to branch, making tweets and whistles that he was sure could be heard throughout the entire forest. He saw a few more cardinals, red males and brownish females, a couple of blue jays that seemed to be chasing each other, and some tiny swifts that zipped up and down along over the path. Trying to follow all of the birds, up in the air and flying every which way, did make Patrick dizzy, to the point where he had to find a log to sit down on and wait until he felt better to continue. He looked around but couldn't find a log, so he decided to simply lean up against the closest tree and rest there until he got his steadiness back. He placed his right hand on the bark of the tree, and balanced himself. After a moment, the dizziness left him and he felt better enough to keep looking for a robin, again. He took his hand off of the bark, taking some pieces off of the tree as they stuck to his hand, and he noticed that his entire palm was covered with tree sap. When he looked closer at the tree, he saw that the entire bottom half of it was practically covered with the sweet and sticky stuff, and the smell of it was evident to him, too. He knelt down to scrape the dirt and bark from his hand, using the leaves of the plants at his feet, when his eyes caught something small and bright blue that was lying on the ground, next to him. As Patrick looked closer, he knew what it was; it was the broken half of a robin's egg. He picked it up, and carefully looked around the ground where his feet were, and when he moved a couple leaves apart from a trufungus plant next to the tree, he found the other half of the egg, in perfect condition. He stood up, holding both halves, and gingerly was able to put them together, making a perfect looking new egg.

But it fell apart into two halves immediately. As he held them in his hand, Patrick thought for a moment then looked up into the branches of the tree, and wedged in there right above him was a nest.

Placing the shell halves back on the ground, Patrick slowly began to climb up the tree, toward the nest. Looking up as he went, he could see the darkening sky through the leaves and branches; he had to hope there was an egg in the nest, grab it and quickly get down the tree and back to his sister as fast as he could. He also noticed two fully grown robins, flying to and from the nest, and he would stop and start his climb as their presence came and went. When he was close enough, and when the birds were not in the nest, he hastened up to it and looked in to find two hatchlings chirping away, with one egg shell that was smashed into many little pieces, and another egg that had not hatched yet, sitting by itself. All he needed to do was grab the egg, get down the tree and hurry out of the forest…and he would be in the clear. However, just as he was about to reach into the nest, the two robin parents returned and landed right in front of him, and Patrick froze, knowing he had been caught in the act of trying to take their egg. He then began to hear voices in his head that said "Please, do not take our egg. It is ready to hatch, and we don't want you to steal it away from us! This is our home, you should not be here!" It was the robins; they were speaking to him, by using their minds, and they looked at Patrick with desperation and kindness, which made him feel incredibly guilty and sad. But he was also bewildered by their communication, and then he remembered what the goblin had told him, about the mystical ways of the forest. He gathered his thoughts for a moment, and then said to them out loud, "I am so sorry to have to do this, but my parents are very sick back home, and the only way to help them is to trade your egg to the goblin in the glen for trufungus weeds that will aid our mother and father. My sister is also under a sleeping spell that the goblin will help break, but only with the egg." The birds answered, "Surely, there must be another way to help your sister and parents, or dealing with the goblin. Please, we beg you; do not take our hatchling-to-be away from us!" Patrick didn't know what to do or say. He felt terrible about having to take the birds' egg away from them, but what else could he do? The goblin wanted nothing else but a robin's egg, and it was too late in the day to climb down the tree and look for another nest in another tree. He stared at the egg, then the hatchlings, then the parents, then back at the egg again, thinking and thinking and thinking…and then he had an idea.

The goblin was down near the creek, under the bridge, trying to catch a fish with his old, wrinkly bare hands, when he heard a voice say "Goblin?! Where are you? I'm back!" It scurried up the little hill, to the end of the bridge, and found Patrick standing over his sister, who was in the exact same spot she was in when he had left, still fast asleep.

"Ah, my lad; How did the exploring go? Did you find what you were looking for in the forest?"

"I did," Patrick answered, and pulled out one of the large trufungus weeds from the tool bag.

"Splendid, my boy; those will do well for your parents. And what about my little request? Were you able to retrieve that, as well?"

Patrick held out his fist, and slowly opened his hand to reveal a blue robin's egg, unbroken and brand new.

"Is this what you wanted?"

"Oh, marvelous! Simply marvelous!" the goblin exclaimed, and reached out to take it from Patrick's hand, but the creature wasn't fast enough, as he moved his hand away before the goblin could snatch it from him.

"Not so fast, goblin! I have your prize, but first you have to help wake my sister from her sleep, and once she is alright, then I will give you the egg."

The goblin was impressed by the boy's newfound confidence, and agreed.

"Of course, young man, you have kept your word, and so I shall do the same-quid pro quo."

The goblin then walked down the other side of the hill, toward the creek, mumbling under his breath, "Delays, delays. Always delays when getting what I want."

Patrick yelled out, "Where are you going? Goblin?? What are doing?!?"

He was about to run after him, when the goblin reappeared from the other side of the bridge.

"Patience, my lad; I had to go find the remedy to your sister's slumber. Take this."

The goblin gave Patrick a large yellow flower that it had brought up from the creek.

"Place this flower under her nose for a moment, and after she breathes in its aroma, she should awaken, full of life and vitality."

Patrick quickly took the flower and ran over to where Shannon was laying, and placed the flower right up against her nose, as to make sure she breathes nothing but the flower for a few seconds, all the while hoping the goblin was right.

"Here, Shannon, breathe this in and please wake up. Please," he said softly to her. Then, miraculously, her eyes opened and she sat up, just as the goblin had said she would.

"Patrick? What happened??"

"You smelled those flowers next to the bridge, and they made you fall asleep for hours," he told her. "I had to go to the forest and get the weeds without you."

"Well done, Patrick! Mother and father will be so proud of you, but we should leave here at once-look how late the day has gotten!"

She stood up and took the tool bag in her hands, then she heard a strange voice that startled her.

"Don't leave just yet, my children. My promise has been kept, now it is time for young Patrick to fulfill his."

Shannon turned around to see the goblin, for the first time, and its appearance frightened her, making her step back and almost lose her footing.

"What are you?"

"Why, my dear, I'm-"

Patrick quickly interrupted them.

"He's the goblin of the glen, and he agreed to help me if I brought back a robin's egg with me. So, here, take it."

He still had the egg in his hand, and walked over to the goblin and carefully placed it in its hand.

"Be careful, I've found they're very fragile. Yes, I know what 'fragile' means," Patrick said to it.

"Oh, my boy, you have done a splendid job, indeed. You are both now free to commence your peregrination home. Do you know what that means? Peregrination?"

Patrick bluntly replied, "We'll ask our parents when we get home. Goodbye, goblin of the glen."

Patrick grabbed his sister's hand, and lead her away from the bridge, back up the hill and onto the pathway that leads back to their home.

The goblin stood there and watched the children as they hastily made their way out of the glen and on their way home, then looked down at its hand and gazed at the blue prize. It began to walk down to the creek, under the bridge, where it would have robin's egg for dinner. Sitting down, the goblin found that it couldn't stop looking at the egg, it was so blue and round, sitting there in its green hand. It then noticed something about the egg; as the goblin looked closer at it, there seemed to be a faint jagged line that went completely around the entire shell, and then the goblin touched the line ever so gently. The egg then split open exactly where the line had been, and the goblin looked to see that there was nothing inside-the egg was empty. That's when it knew the boy had fooled him. The creature lifted the egg up to its shriveled nose, and could smell the sweet aroma of tree sap. The boy had found an empty eggshell, perfectly halved, and stuck the two sides together with the sap, making it look like a perfectly solid egg. The goblin, thinking back on its conversation with the boy, remembered saying it wanted a robin's egg, but didn't say it couldn't be empty. A fully intact egg was implied, but never agreed upon by the two parties. The young boy had fooled it, and that was a lesson to be learned, the goblin sighed in disappointment, as it tossed the two shell halves over its shoulder, and then dove into the water, looking for a fish that it could have for dinner.

STAR SEEDS

(or Invaders From Mars, PA)

In 2004, the Rosetta space probe was launched from the Guiana
Space Centre in South America, on a mission to intercept, orbit and
study the Comet Churyumov-Gerasimenko (67P), carrying with it
the Philae landing module, which the probe was going to set down
on to the comet's surface, in order to collect samples and return
data to Earth to enhance our understanding of its composition,
origin and possibly gain information regarding space, in general.
The mission, which lasted over twelve years, was a historic success,
with the probe and Philae module sending back data that detected
organic molecules in the comet's atmosphere and on its surface,
among hundreds of other details that took scientists years to
scrutinize and correlate. These accomplishments led to subsequent
missions to other celestial bodies, one of which was the launch of the
Webster/Steed probe, five years after the conclusion of the Rosetta
mission. The Webster/Steed probe carried with it the Astraea landing
module, and they were sent on a ten-year mission to intercept the
Comet Shulman-Borofsky (87C), which is a remnant of the Beta
Scorpiids meteor cluster. The probe's task was to intercept and orbit
87C as it passed between Jupiter and Mars (perilously close to the
solar system's Main Asteroid Belt), while sending the Astraea to the
surface, mirroring the Philae's mission over a decade earlier;
however, technology had been developed and built into the Astraea
that would allow it to take off from the comet's surface, rendezvous
back with the probe and have both separate from 87C's trajectory,
in order to return to Earth, bringing with them a plethora of physical
samples as well as scientific data that, once studied, could possibly

reveal an encyclopedia of secrets to our galaxy, and set a precedent for future space exploration. The mission's execution was flawless, and the probe was preparing to re-enter the Earth's atmosphere for its final descent towards the Atlantic Ocean, until...

The fiery remnants of the domestic spacecraft came bursting through the midnight rain and clouds, glowing like the tails of a huge firework display, and landed at the edge of a field, at the far end of the immense Harris farm, which ran parallel with the Allegheny Forest. The forest separated the farm from the city limits of the small Western Pennsylvania town of Mars, which was currently experiencing a citywide blackout due to the massive electrical storm that had settled over the area earlier that evening. As the burning wreckage lay in pieces on the rain soaked meadow, the flames were quickly extinguished, leaving various pieces of metal strewn next to the tree line of the forest. Among the debris was a metal container that had broke open upon impact with the ground, and its contents were now scattered among the rest of the debris - countless tiny charcoal-colored pellets that littered the moist ground, along with a copious amount of black dirt, that one would say resembled space soot. The electrical storm seemed to gather strength overhead, and lightening began to strike down onto the crash site in a violent barrage of white bolts, hitting the contents of the container and electrifying everything on the ground, acting like a superconductor, allowing the electric shock to affect the entire area, including the vegetation of the field and forest. Nearby trees were also struck, their bark and limbs exploding into thousands of pieces that flew off in every direction. On the ground, the pellets were glowing from the lightening strike, with steam rising from their surfaces, and then they slowly began to seep into the ground, becoming buried underneath the mud and puddles. The rain continued to fall, even as the storm rolled on out of the area, the thunder getting more and more faint and quiet as the early morning hours approached.

It had been a challenging Friday night for Mitch Harris, to say the least. Between the cacophony of the storm and the constant movement of his six year-old sleeping daughter, who had been so scared by the storm that she literally jumped into bed with him and his wife, Cindy, he didn't get much sleep. He checked the time on his cell phone when he finally got out of bed to use the bathroom - 6:09a.m. – and when he was finished, he knew he couldn't go back to bed. Whatever wrath the storm had left, Mitch new the sooner he went to inspect the damage, the sooner it could be cleaned up and the farm's regular chores could be tended to. It wasn't a big farm, but it did have its fair share of maintenance: lawn care, a few animals to feed, and decent sized garden to work on, not to mention a pool on the side of the house that needed cleaning. He shuddered to think of what could have landed in the pool during the night; the last big storm had left two drowned bats, a shit ton of leaves and branches and half the patio furniture in the water, and he remembers what a bitch it was cleaning that mess up. God only knows what was waiting for him this morning.

On a positive note, the storm had completely cleared out, and now there was a clear blue sky and glorious bright sunshine that rose over the farm and the rest of Mars. Mitch was shocked to find that only a few leaves had made their way into the pool (with nothing dead in it, either), so he felt that task could wait and be handled by his fifteen year-old son, Michael, and decided to pull the riding mower out of the garage to take a trip around the property, hoping the rest of it was as undamaged as the pool. He cruised by the small barn and yard, where their two small horses, goat and three chickens resided, and saw that all of them were out and about. He decided he would just drive around the perimeter fence for now, and worry about a fuller inspection of the property later, when he was actually using the mower to cut the grass, which he was putting off until tomorrow, allowing for everything to dry out in the sun today…he loathed cutting and cleaning off wet grass!

Driving around the property, not really seeing any damage or debris to be concerned with, Mitch began to think about how badly they needed the rain and storm last night. It had been a dry start to the summer, and his landscaping business, which had flourished practically year-round for the past eight years, was beginning to see a slowdown in work, some of it due to the weather and some due to competition that had sprung up over the past couple of years. Mars wasn't that large of a community, and it certainly was big enough to accommodate more than three or four landscaping businesses…successfully, anyway. The irony was he had hoped the storm would have lasted longer, but a little rain is better than nothing. He was approaching the far end of his property, about a hundred yards away from the house and against the Allegheny Forest tree line, and was getting ready to turn around and head back, when he pulled up to the crash site. There was an immense fluttering of activity all over the area, which was partly burned out by the fire that the crash has caused, and partly covered by a growth of new, and incredibly large, dandelion and butter flower plants that had never been there before; this part of his land was mostly all tall grass and weeds. The beauty of the large flowers had a stark contrast of appearance against the black scorched dirt they had grown out of. Mitch stopped the tractor, stepped onto the muddy ground and slowly took a look around the flora-filled wreckage, but it wasn't easy, because with the newly arrived plants came a plethora of birds and insects who were quickly taking advantage of the abundant food source that had blossomed. He stood still, letting his eyes do the reconnoitering: the ground was colonized with earthworms, who the birds (robins, mostly) were also having a field day with, and the metallic remnants of the module, which were strewn all over the place, charred black from the heat of the burning descent and subsequent impact explosion. Mitch reached down and picked up a small rectangular piece of steel at his feet, wiped what mud and soot he could off of it, and was able to make out the words "specimen box" written in black print lettering across the one side. He then looked up at the virtual feeding frenzy that was taking place, spying a couple of cardinals fighting each other in midflight, over a very long worm that one of them had dangling from its beak, and while he followed them through the air, Mitch caught the sight of a fruit bat, hanging in one of the trees, observing the whole scene, as well. He continued scanning the area, noticing the large number of bees that had arrived along with the birds, and thought it might be a good idea to depart and come back after a while, after things calmed down a bit. He hopped back up onto the tractor, took a second to snap a picture of the scene on his cell phone so he could show everyone back home, turned the vehicle around and drove back to the house. Looking at his home, off in the distance, the thought of all the strange activity he had just seen was replaced by a mental to-do list for the day, as well as remembering that he had to help out with his son's baseball practice that weekend, and he wondered if the fields would dry out by then.

Two days later…

It was a beautiful sunset, Maggie thought, looking out the kitchen window that sat over the sink, where she and Michael were washing and drying the dishes from dinner. The view out of the window was of the backyard, then the Butler County forest beyond that, where the sun had disappeared twenty minutes earlier, and now the sky was a rainbow of blue, orange, peach, pink and a tinge of purple that signaled to her the coming of a clear and starry night. "A rainbow sherbet sunset. Isn't it beautiful, honey?" Michael was drying the plates next to her and putting them up in the cabinet above where he was standing, and glanced out the window. "Oh yeah, sweet." He probably would have appreciated the sight more if he were outside in the yard, not stuck inside holding a damp towel, but Maggie enjoyed his response, nonetheless. "By the way," he continued, "I think Heather and I are going to try to get tickets for the Bucs game on Wednesday; they're playing Cincy, and she likes one of their players. I love competing with a professional athlete." His mother laughed and said, "Oh, honey, she just has a crush. Don't take it personally." Speaking of crushes, she peered out the window, into the yard at her husband, who still gave her butterflies almost every time she looked at him. Mitch had gone outside to check on the horses by the barn, which had started to make noises right after the family had finished eating, and almost simultaneously as the sun went down. The window had been open to let the evening breeze into the kitchen, so it was easy to hear the clamor when it started out in the yard, and Mitch felt it was necessary to go out and investigate the situation, thinking maybe another animal was in the forest and had spooked them; they hadn't seen a fox or coyote in a while, but every now and then one would try to sneak onto the property and the horses didn't approve of that. Maggie could see Mitch out by the barn, holding onto one of the horses, while the other one galloped around the yard, from one side of the brown wooden fence back to the barn and then to the fence again, almost in a frantic pace now, and she hoped Mitch wouldn't get hurt trying to calm it down.

Mitch couldn't understand why the horse was behaving this way, and he thought if he could get the one he was holding on to safely back in the barn, he would then call for Michael to help corral the other one. He felt that something definitely must have scared it, but he looked around the yard and couldn't see anything that would have intimidated or frightened the animal. As he walked to the front of the barn, which faced the forest, he could now hear noises coming from deep in the woods, and it sounded like someone was cutting down trees and snapping off limbs and branches from their trunks. He said out loud to himself, "Who the hell would be working in the forest at this hour? And why?? That's insane!" The questions didn't linger long in his mind, because at that moment he felt a large gust of wind from overhead knock him down onto the ground. Dirt had kicked up into his eyes, and when he was able to get a clear view through the dust cloud that the gust had created, he saw the horse he had been standing next to, now being raised up into the air by a giant fruit bat, which was twice the size of animal. Its feet had dug into the body of the horse, and it flapped its wings rapidly and with incredible power, allowing it to carry the panic-stricken horse straight up into the air. More grass and dirt kicked up into Mitch's face, as he struggled to stand up and watch as the bat easily carried its prize off into the darkness over the forest, the horse's neighing and screeching fading in the distance.

Mitch stood there in shock and bewilderment, frozen in fear that there might be more bats that size out there, waiting to attack in the same manner as that one just did. Standing there, contemplating what to do next, he then turned to get back to the house and his family, when the ground began to shake violently, like an earthquake was beginning. "Now an earthquake?!?" he yelled. "That's not possible!" Struggling to keep his balance, he heard the rest of the animals in the barn going nuts, and they all came rushing out of the doors, into the yard, when a large boom came from inside the barn, and a second later, the head of a giant earthworm exploded through the roof of the barn, thrusting itself skyward before falling horizontal to the ground, crushing the side of the barn and shaking the earth, again, as it landed hard on to two of the chickens, right in front of Mitch. The worm was enormous, and he could smell an oozy odor that emanated from its body. The creature, not seeming to have any eyes, turned its huge head and large, circular mouth toward Mitch, as it gave out a disturbing growl that made him cover his ears in protection. The second horse then darted in front of him, and the worm wasted no time lunging for it, and snatched it into its mouth in one motion. This gave Mitch a second to think, and he immediately darted through the yard, up to the house.

Inside, Maggie had seen everything that was happening, first through the window, and then when she ran to the backdoor and screamed for Mitch to get inside. As she watched as the worm ate the horse and Mitch started to run up through the yard, the house violently shook, and she was knocked back against the wall opposite the door, and the floor in front of her burst apart, as the head of another giant worm came crashing up into the kitchen! Tile flew everywhere, as the worm roared and flung its body around the room, crushing cabinets and counters, as well as the sink, which was completely destroyed, and now water came bursting through the exposed pipes, flooding the kitchen floor. Michael, who had been putting dishes away on the other side of the room when all hell broke loose, yelled for his mother to get out of there, but she was trapped against the far back wall. She yelled back, telling him to go find his sister and to get out of the house as fast as possible. He rushed out of the kitchen, through the dining room to the front of the house, and ran upstairs to Cindy's room, where he found her crouching in a corner, crying and frozen in fear. "C'mon! We have to leave, NOW!!" He grabbed her arm and pulled her to her feet, then led her out of the room and back to the stairs. But before they could run down and out the front door, another worm came crashing up through the staircase, destroying their escape route. Michael thought quickly, and led them back to his room and over to the window, which he opened and they both climbed out and onto the roof of the garage. He planned on them either jumping down off of the roof, onto their father's pickup truck that was sitting in the driveway, or at worst maybe jumping into the pool, which was right next to the garage.

Meanwhile, Mitch couldn't get into the house from the backyard now, seeing how the worm inside the kitchen had demolished the backdoor, so he was forced to go around the side of the house and try to get to his family from the front. He ran through the yard, picking up a pitchfork that was laying on the ground in front of him that must have been thrown from the barn, and continued ahead until he heard a loud buzzing from above, which made him abruptly stop in his tracks; he had to see what the source of the sound was, so he slowly turned and looked up to see a humongous bumblebee hovering about ten feet above him. His mouth was gaped open in literal awe for a moment, but then instinct kicked in as he turned and sprinted to the side of the house, with the bee chasing him overhead. As he sprinted through the yard, he could hear the bee's buzzing, which sounded like a huge generator hovering over his head, getting closer and louder. He then felt a large push on his shoulders, and fell to the ground, rolling over a couple of times, and finally stopping with his back against the ground, as he stared up and the large insect as it swooped down upon him. He could feel its many legs grab at him, around his torso and chest, and they tightened their hold with such force that he could feel the air leave his lungs, as it lifted him off of the ground. Fortunately, he was able to maintain his grip on the pitchfork with his right hand, and he began to repeatedly stab at the bee's rotund body as fast as he could, not wanting to get too far into the air…it would be a helluva fall back to terra firma. Ooze started to flow from its body, falling onto the tool's handle and over Mitch's hand and arm, and the bee gave off a loud yelp of pain then released him from its grip, dropping him back to Earth, as he had hoped and feared. He landed with a hard thud, which knocked what little wind he had left out of him. The wounded bee flew off towards the forest, leaving a stream of ooze on the ground, all the way back to the woods. Mitch regained his breath, staggered to his feet and glanced back to the yard in time to see the giant worm snatch their goat up with its circular mouth and swallow it whole. Screams were coming from inside the house that caught his attention, and he sprinted through the patch of lawn that ran down the side of the house and led to the front yard, hoping he could safely enter from there.

Michael was getting ready to help Cindy get off of the garage roof by lowering her down onto the hood of their father's heavy duty pickup in the driveway. It would be a drop of a few feet, but they had no choice but to go this route. Before they could start, however, they both heard the sound of flapping wings overhead, and looked up to see a huge cardinal descending toward them, itself screeching out of its large, sword-like beak. The bird's feathers weren't the usual bright red color, but a dirty crimson and brownish now, and they noticed that its head seemed deformed, looking like a menacing, demonic bird from hell. It stretched out its clawed feet to try to snatch them both from the roof, but Michael, with Cindy behind him, swept the feet away with his arms; this went on for a minute, with the bird coming back at Michael more aggressively each time, trying to get its claws around him. His shirt became shredded from the force of contact with the sharp talons, and Cindy, watching as she crouched behind him, knew she had to get down to the truck as fast as possible, so she leapt out from behind Michael, jumped into the air and landed on top of the roof of the cab, with her momentum carrying her off of that and into the bed of the truck. She felt pain shoot up her legs from her feet, as she tumbled onto the plastic bed liner, stopping against the back of the tailgate, and letting out her own cry of pain, catching the attention of the possessed bird. When it saw her writhing in pain down in the truck bed, the cardinal left Michael and flew up and over the driveway. Cindy was crying, holding her left ankle and yelling Michael's name as the bird landed on the truck, grabbed her with its sharp feet, and lifted her out of the truck bed. Michael watched in horror as his sister cried, screamed and struggled to get loose of the bird's grasp, and it looked at him one last time before flying up and over his head, then disappearing into the starry night sky. All he could do was stand there and weep, his heart dropping to his stomach, feeling helpless, guilty and confused over what just happened. At that moment, he felt a sharp painful stabbing of something sharp hit him from behind and cut right through his back and out his chest, as a long black stinger, looking like a huge dark needle, burst through the front of his body. He instinctively grabbed at it with both hands, as blood and fluid began flowing out of his mouth and chest, and his head fell backward, allowing him to see the rest of the giant hornet on top of him; it looked like it was as large as the truck in the driveway, and his hair flew all around due to the rapid wing movement of the insect as it picked the teen up off of the roof and high into the air, just like the bird did with Cindy. They flew over the swimming pool, and at that moment, with Michael angled down toward the ground, gravity took over and he slid out of the hold of the fluid-soaked stinger, and fell motionless and facedown into the water. The impact was enough to knock him unconscious, as blood began to surround his floating, motionless body. The hornet flew down to retrieve its prey, but before it could reach the pool, an enormous brown bat, which was twice the size of the hornet, swooped in out of nowhere, snatched Michael's body out of the water with its large fang-toothed mouth, and flew off as fast as it had arrived, as a surprised and angry hornet chased after it, both disappearing in the dark nocturnal abyss.

Inside the house, Maggie had found temporary refuge in their dining room, after leaping through a hole in the wall that separated it from the kitchen, created when the worm wildly crashed through it during its attack. Now, it was stuck floundering in the kitchen, apparently caught in the piping underneath the sink and dishwasher, and she took this time to gather her faculties; she flipped the dining room table on its side and pushed it up against the wall, covering up most of the hole…would it help? Probably not, but it made her feel a little safer, either way. She could hear the other worm (the one that had burst through the stairs) clamoring about on the other side of the house, in the living room, she guessed. She could also now see the front door from where she was at, looking through the dining room and past the adjacent family room, which was the one place that seemed untouched by the mayhem, to this point. However, Maggie also noticed there was a lot of debris in front of the doorway, and she wondered how difficult it would be to traverse all of that and actually exit with any sort of haste, while also not garnering the attention of any of the worms. After contemplating her limited choices for a brief couple of seconds, she made up her mind to sprint through the two rooms, to the front door, and just hope that she could open it quickly enough to get out before her escape was detected.

Mitch had made his way to the front yard, where he could hear the destruction occurring inside his house, with the noise of shattering glass, collapsing walls and the smashing of furniture, among the cacophony of growls and shrieks of the giant worms that had burrowed their way into their home. He desperately wanted to find Maggie and the kids, not knowing their fates at the moment; all he knew was that he had to get into the house, someway, to find anyone if they were still in there, and get them to safety. Mitch was by himself in the front yard, as no deformed and overgrown wildlife had made it to this part of the property yet, and that bought him a few moments to decide on a plan of entry and some sort of reconnaissance, once inside the house. Taking a step toward the front porch, he then noticed a shadow moving slowly around, down the side of the house, where he had just come from. He took a few guarded steps back, looking deep into the shaded grassy area, and then he froze in his tracks. Out of the darkness and stepping into the front yard (and the brightness of the porch floodlight, that was somehow still magically illuminating the entire front of the property), was a sight that made Mitch's heart drop to his stomach. It was a coyote, but just like the worms and the bee, it was larger than normal. In fact, he guessed that it was the size of a grizzly bear, with an enlarged head and snout that seemed to have been grotesquely deformed by their rapid increases in size, Mitch thought, as it slowly crept toward him. It had a slow, baritone growl that made Mitch's hairs stand on end, and he could now see chicken feathers and blood falling from its gaping mouth, with the flood light glistening off of its oversized, exposed fangs. During this stare down, both of them had drifted to the center of the front yard, with about 25 feet between, and the coyote had maneuvered itself to a spot that put it closer to the front porch than Mitch was, but if he ran fast enough, he could at least make a B-line to the truck in the driveway, which he was closer to and where Mitch hoped he could find some defilade there. It then occurred to him that an aluminum baseball bat sat in the equipment bag that was still in the truck bed from Michael's baseball practice the day before.

He looked at the truck, then quickly back at the beastly canine, and then took a stutter step to his left, making the coyote lurch forward in that direction, while Mitch made like a jackrabbit toward the truck, off to his right. The coyote slipped a bit in the grass, trying to change directions as Mitch darted past the sidewalk that split the yard in half, and he knew he had a good head start on the thing. However, its size and power quickly made up for its mistake, and it bounded toward Mitch, who knew he only had one shot at getting into the truck bed before its teeth and claws would be on him. He could hear it growling louder, and sweat fell into his eyes from his forehead as he reached the driveway and took a diving leap into the air, at the same time as the beast was leaping at him. It managed to only swipe at his lower left leg, as Mitch flew over the side of the truck and landed in the bed, and the coyote landed head first into the side of the truck with such force that the truck shifted its position in the driveway, and a large dent was left where its head and body had slammed into the vehicle. Mitch practically landed on the black equipment bag, and immediately opened it and reached in for the bat. The stunned coyote lifted its head up and over the side of the truck, still growling and snarling at Mitch, spitting saliva, feathers and blood all over the truck bed. It lunged for him with its sharp teeth, but it only grabbed the equipment bag, which it yanked away from Mitch with one swift turn of its head, and baseball paraphernalia flew off out of the bag, in every direction. The bat, however, was already secure in Mitch's grasp, and when the coyote turned back to Mitch, he was already in mid-swing and landed a direct hit to the side of the beast's head; teeth and spit also went flying in every direction. He continued to hit it in rapid succession, crushing its skull against the top of the truck bed, until it stopped moving and fell onto the concrete driveway. Mitch stood up and looked at the body of the huge beast, lying motionless next to the truck, in utter amazement at its immense size.

Maggie then came running out of the front door and down the porch stairs, onto the sidewalk and was about to head for the street, when Mitch yelled to her as loud as he could. "Maggie! Wait!" She stopped half way between the house and the street, turning to see Mitch standing in the back of the truck, and softly said out loud, "Mitch?" He jumped down to the ground as she began to run over to him, when one of the worms came crashing out through the living room window and wall, landing in the yard directly behind Maggie, who had reached the driveway and fell into her husband's arms. "What the hell is happening, Mitch??" she exclaimed, with a fear in her voice that he never thought he would hear. "I don't know," he replied, "but we have to get the hell out of here! Where are the kids??" "I have no idea," she said, now almost crying at the thought of what could have happened to Michael and Cindy. Mitch knew they had no time to worry about the kids, unfortunately, because the worm had turned in their direction, shrieking through the air with an ear-piercing sound that made both of them cover their ears, and Mitch then grabbed Maggie's hand and started to lead her down the driveway, when the second worm came smashing out of the garage, sending its door up into the air and out into the yard, striking the other worm on its head. It pushed the pick-up truck easily out of its way and back down the driveway, just behind the fleeing couple, who were now running down the street in the direction of the neighboring Mars Memorial Cemetery, which bordered their property to the south.

Their dead-end street stopped right at the edge of the cemetery, and the couple raced through the small row of trees and bushes that separated the properties, and practically fell into the graveyard. Both were breathing heavy and sweating profusely, and Maggie nearly dropped to her knees in exhaustion, but Mitch caught her as she collapsed into his arms, again. "C'mon, babe," he whispered into her ear with both caring and urgency. "We can't stop. I don't hear them back there, anymore - and that worries me." Mitch knew that on the other side of the cemetery was a dirt road that led to Evans City Blvd., which they could take into town, where hopefully their kids will know to head to, as well, and their family would safely be reunited. "Hey, Maggie?" He asked, as he stood her up and held her face in his hands. "We need to just get to Evans City, and take that into town. I know the kids will find us there." With tears in her eyes, she nodded and said, "Yeah, ok. I'm ready." Mitch wiped her face clean, as she took a long deep breath, grabbed his hand and they swiftly jogged through the cemetery, over and past headstones and gravesites, until they were about halfway through when a new noise was heard overhead. Stopping out of caution, they looked up to see the giant brown bat and hornet engaged in a violent aerial fight, the noise being the cries of the bat as it flapped about in a circular motion, both attacking and being attacked by the huge insect. "Keep moving! Keep moving!" Mitch yelled, taking the lead and pulling Maggie faster through the graveyard. "Wait, Mitch! Wait!" She yanked back on his arm, pointing over to their left, on the ground, where she could see Michael's body, lying face up and motionless.

"Michael!" she screamed, and both parents rushed to his side, seeing that his eyes were closed, and there was blood coming out of his mouth. Maggie knelt down, leaning over his head, trying to see if he was breathing. "No, no, no. Michael! Can you hear me, honey??" She was frantic, now, her hands shaking and tears flowing down her face, again. Mitch, simply in shock at the site of his son, who seemed fatally injured by whatever had attacked him, looked over his son's body, seeing the crimson-stained hole in his shirt, and whose clothes were completely soaked. "What…what could have happened?" Mitch said in pure disbelief. "They killed him!" Maggie answered. "They killed our son, Mitch!" She fell over her son's head, which she cradled now in her lap, weeping and crying hysterically.

Mitch began to think about Cindy's fate, and felt so weak in the knees that he had to sit down on top of a headstone that was a few feet away. Just as he did, the two flying creatures came crashing to the ground about twenty yards away from them, still battling with the bat on top of the hornet, swatting at it with its humongous wings. He watched the battle continue for a moment, when the earth began to shake all around them, and then the two worms came bursting out of the ground behind them, tossing caskets and headstones wildly all over the graveyard. Mitch instinctively jumped over to Maggie and their son, throwing his arms and body over them both, as dirt and grass came crashing all about them; a long black coffin landed a few feet away from them, landing top down and shattering in a hundred pieces, but not before tossing its skeletal contents all over the three of them. Maggie screamed so loud that Mitch's ears began to ring; he wiped the dirt and dust from his eyes, and turned around to see the worms quickly crawling over in their direction, fighting off each other in a sort of race to see who could reach the humans first. Knowing their fate was sealed, at this point, all he could do was to cover up Maggie and send up a prayer for their daughter, as he closed his eyes and quietly said to his wife, "Keep holding Michael, baby. Don't look up-just keep holding Michael. We're together now, everything will be okay."

JUNKYARD AL

Today was one of those days where everything was saturated with perspiration. Driving around the northeast corner of the San Fernando Valley, in the middle of August, in a beat up 1980 GMC pick-up truck, with no air conditioning or power-anything, was Josh's definition of *miserable*. Whoever has the distinction of coming up with the term "valley heat" must have been working a manual labor job that required long pants, thick boots, gloves and (usually) a long sleeve shirt. He typically wore a t-shirt underneath, so Josh would routinely remove the outer garment at midday, which cooled things off a bit, but he still would sweat like a whore in church. A t-shirt was a small consolation when dealing with triple digit temps, and while driving around at speeds of 50-60 mph, with the windows down, helped keep his upper half somewhat comfortable (especially in the morning hours), every inch of his body cooked like a turkey on Thanksgiving in the afternoons. Southern California is not known for its humidity, but a few times a year it experiences a fair share of sticky weather, and add high temperatures to that, and you end up in Josh's current state of sweating bullets from head to toe. Even his Target-bought trucker's cap-the one with the rooster patch on the front-was soaked through, while his old Metallica "Ride the Lightening" tee was sticking to his skin like masking tape. Sitting in the cab, his back felt like it was just laying in a pool of warm water, sinking into the seat as if it was a wet patio cushion that had been left out in the rain all day.

He was driving to a junkyard in aptly named Sun Valley, CA, to drop off a large haul of scrap and, well…junk, that he had collected over the past three days while cruising the residential streets of the SFV, from west in Thousand Oaks over to Sylmar, where he was now coming from, stalking neighborhoods off of the 101, 118, 170 and 5 freeways. He would collect and haul whatever he could find laying out on curbs, in trash bins and dumpsters, front yards, you name it. If it fit in his truck bed, he took it. This particular delivery wasn't a bad haul; he had a decent amount of stuff to drop off, but he was disappointed that it had taken three days to collect it all. He usually liked to go only one or two days between drops, but this week had started out slow, so he was forced to wait an extra day to make the trip back to the 'yard. He drove down San Fernando Road and turned into the driveway, pulling up and underneath a large grey sign with black lettering that read "Jesús' Junkyard" that hung above the gated entrance, and he always chuckled when he saw this. He honked the truck's horn quickly twice, and a moment later, the gate rolled open to his right, and the yard's usual employee who worked the entrance waved to him to come inside. "Hola, Juan," Josh said as he drove by him. "Hey hey, Junkyard Josh is back!" yelled Juan, in a thick Mexican accent that complimented his short, rotund appearance. Juan's apparel was similar to Josh's: pants, shirt, ball cap, boots. But Juan had his dark Latino skin, black mustache and thick black hair underneath the hat, which contrasted Josh's long, stringy blonde hair, blue eyes and white Irish skin, although the dirt and grit from working all day helped enough to bring his color a little closer to his ethnic friend's.

Juan directed the truck back into the lot, along the gravel and pothole covered driveway, which made the truck rock back and forth like a boat on rough seas. Josh drove past a small office building and toward a large blue empty metal container. He parked next to it, and a couple other Mexican gentlemen unloaded the contents of his truck bed and placed it all in the container, while Josh stayed inside the cab. After a few minutes, Juan, who had been standing next to a large scale display, wrote on the clipboard he was carrying, and came over to Josh, and handed the board him. Josh signed the weight receipt that was attached to it, and Juan walked away, into the office building, and returned a couple of minutes later, and presented Josh with a plain white envelope, and politely said, "There you go, amigo. Adios!" "Gracias, Juanito. Adios." Juan laughed, and Josh drove off of the scales, turned around in the large dirt patch that separated the weigh-in area from the rest of the yard, and proceeded back the way he came in, where Juan had walked back to and opened the gate so he could exit. The entire visit took about ten minutes, tops. Three days of doing all that driving and work, and he was in and out of there like that. Actually, that was the best part of the job. He really didn't want to spend more time in that place than he had to, so ten minutes was just fine with him. Now all he had to do was go to the bank, deposit his check, and then sit in rush hour traffic driving home. His bank was a half-mile down the road, and he was able to park right in front and get an ATM immediately. He got out of the truck and stretched his legs, since it felt like he had been in there for a week, and took his time walking up to the machine, enjoying a slight breeze that made him stop and look up at the crystal blue, cloudless sky. He finished a bottle of water he had opened when leaving the yard, and threw it away in a trashcan next to the ATM. He stood there and tried to separate his wet clothes from his skin, went up and deposited the $200 check, while also withdrawing twenty bucks, then got back into the truck. Before leaving, he took out another bottle of water from his cooler in the front seat, then put the cassette of Van Halen's '5150' album in the stereo, cranked it up, took a big swig of agua and headed toward the freeway.

Outside of its hauling capabilities, the only redeeming quality the truck had was its stereo. Josh had an old Pioneer cassette stereo and speakers installed in it as soon as he bought it, which was eight years ago, and the stereo never failed him. The stereo was also the only good thing about his vehicle prior to the truck, which had been a 1980 silver Voyager van that he drove for almost ten years. The bad thing about the van was that the speakers were way in the back, so volume was always an issue, since most of the music was coming out six feet behind him (the van's own speakers, in the dash up front, were underwhelming, at best). With the pick-up, however, he was able to install the speakers right behind the front seat, which made an incredible audio difference. Especially listening to the Van Halen tapes; it didn't matter that they were all the original cassettes he had bought way back, because the stereo gave them a killer sound. And since Eddie's guitar was almost always in the left stereo channel, that placed his ax work directly behind Josh's ears while driving…rock and roll heaven! For Josh, it didn't matter who was singing; whether it was Roth, Hagar or Gary Cherone in his one-off stint on VH III – it was all about the music, for him. All of his friends knew he was a huge VH fan, and when asked about his favorite album, he would always say it was a tie, between 1984 and 5150; those two records he felt epitomized the best qualities of both the Roth and Hagar incarnations of the band, both musically and lyrically. He would also never get sucked into an argument over the selection of Cherone as Sammy's replacement in 1998, or the drama and mudslinging that historically seemed to follow the band no matter what direction they went in with a front man. Josh wouldn't hear of it, he would not be beguiled into any negative or cynical opinions of the band or its music.

As the beginning of 'Best of Both Worlds' cranked through his speakers, he pulled off of the freeway and down the Oxnard exit instead of the usual Burbank exit, because of the latter being closed for CalTrans work. This wasn't a problem, since he could just detour down a few side streets and back track to his rented house on Beck Street. In doing so, he drove passed a few North Hollywood houses that had some junk laying out on the curb, and he was more than happy to briefly stop, leave the truck on, and hurriedly toss the items in the back: a rusty tricycle, a medium-sized and heavier-than-it-looked trunk (for clothes, he assumed) and a metal twin bed frame that was in two pieces and fit perfectly in the bed of the truck. The trunk was the last thing he stopped for, and as soon as he drove away, the worst thing that could possibly happen, happened: the cassette stopped playing and the stereo shut off…disaster! He tried to eject the tape, but it was stuck in there. Within seconds he pulled into his driveway, and thought maybe it was a fuse, but checked them and found all were still good. Now he was super bummed. Losing both a prized tape and the stereo was a wicked double blow that immediately put him in a bad mood. He didn't even feel like dealing with the junk he had just put in the truck; he just wanted to go inside, cook some dinner and think of how he could fix the stereo, without destroying it or the cassette.

He walked in the house through the side door, off of the driveway, that led right into the kitchen, where he went straight for the freezer and took out a box of chicken fried rice and threw it in the microwave. Hitting "Quick Cook" and then "3", the microwave turned on and began to cook the frozen dinner, as he went back to the fridge and took out a can of beer, then opened the freezer again and removed a glass that immediately frosted up and into which he poured his drink. He took a nice long drink, and halfway through it, the microwave shutoff, as did the kitchen light that he flicked on when he got home. He walked over and opened the door to find his dinner not even thawed out yet. "What the hell is going on," he said out loud. He went into the living room and turned on the ceiling light in there, but it wouldn't come on, either. He let out a frustrated "AAAWWW" and went down the hallway, to the fuse box on the wall, and saw that all were still on, so he had no idea what the problem was. He checked all of the light switches in the house, and none of them worked. Out of desperation, he grabbed his cell phone off of the kitchen counter and decided to call a buddy, who happened to be an electrician. But as soon as he dialed the number, the phone died. Josh was beside himself; not only was he starving and badly in need of a shower, he now had no power for anything electrical around him. He decided to go outside and check to see if the neighbors had power, or if the whole street was out. It was barely dusk, so there was still some daylight illuminating the neighborhood, but he could hear the house next door's air conditioner going, and street lights had just came on, as well, so whatever was wrong was isolated on him.

Josh walked down the driveway and got into the truck, deciding to drive over to Del Taco and eat something and take time to gather his thoughts about the situation. He went to start the pick-up and…nada. Now his truck wouldn't start; there was no power at all from the battery, so he was completely powerless, literally. He got out, slammed the driver's door shut and went to go back into the house when he heard a bumping noise occur from the truck bed, and he froze in his tracks. He thought maybe an animal had jumped in the back, and had perhaps smelled something in the trunk and was trying to get it open, so he cautiously approached the back of it and lowered the gate to reveal nothing back there, just the trunk, bed frame and bike. Then he heard another bump, and noticed the trunk shake and move slightly, so apparently there was something inside that he now had to deal with, on top of being put back in the Stone Age. He carefully took the trunk out of the back of the truck, and again it shook from inside as he placed it on the driveway's concrete surface, where it sat still for just a couple seconds only to begin shaking again, more violently this time. Boldly and with a sense of urgency, Josh unlocked the clasp in the front of it and opened the bulky lid, lifting it up and back, and he peered inside to find a creature that he had never seen before, nor could he immediately think of words to describe what it even looked like. The thing made a sound like a chirp and growl mixed together, which caused Josh to quickly shut the lid and take a step back. He paused for a moment, then he picked up the trunk and scuttled into the house with it, all the while hearing the thing inside making the same chirp/growl noise.

Josh almost tripped through the side door, trying to carry the trunk and close the door at a speed that you shouldn't move at while attempting both of those tasks. He placed the trunk on top of the coffee table in the middle of the darkened living room, grabbed a match and lit a votive candle on the fireplace mantle and placed it at the corner of the table. The room's main window was directly behind the couch, where he now sat, staring at the trunk in front of him and listening to the noises that the thing was making inside. He thought about what he had seen, and it did remind him of something he had seen before, but he couldn't quite place it, yet. After a couple of fast, successive chirps, Josh stopped thinking about opening the box and just did it. He slowly lifted and brought the lid down onto the table, peered inside, and looking at the dark skinned being again, he knew immediately what it looked like: it reminded him of the animated grease spot that appears during the opening credits of the movie *Grease*. Yep, that was it he thought, as he stared down at this thing, and it at him, with two large eyes that sat on top of its body like white saucers with black centers, sans eyelids, and making those noises through a mouth that opened like an upside down mud flap.

As bizarre as it all seemed, Josh found himself surprisingly calm and accepting of his current situation, that which being a new adoptive parent to what he had to guess was an alien. So, he only found it natural and appropriate that he name his new friend, and the name he immediately came up with was Al. Al the Alien. Junkyard Al…it had a ring to it, even though he didn't find it in a j-yard, but it didn't matter. He noticed that Al seemed to want out of the trunk (hey, who wouldn't?), so Josh gently moved the trunk back to the edge of the coffee table, making room in the front of it for Al. "Okay, bud. It's cool to climb out, now. If that's what you want to do, I'm guessing." He sat there looking at the outside of the box and table bathed in the fading light through the window behind him, and after a few seconds, Al slid his purple-black body up over the edge and down the front of the trunk, slowly landing on top of the table, and moved around so that it and Josh were facing each other. The movement of its body looked like the toy ooze that novelty stores sold, and since Al had no problem with gravity as he moved up and down the sides of the trunk, his skin must have an adhering quality to it, to help him stick to vertical surfaces. "Uh, hello - I'm Josh," he said to it, as if he were introducing himself to a blind date. Al just looked at him. No eyelids, so it didn't blink-just stared, which was weird to Josh. "This is my home. We're in North Hollywood, California." Seriously, what the hell do you say to an alien? It didn't make any noises in response, but began to look around the living room, and then its eyesight landed on the candle at the corner of the coffee table, and seemed to become fixated with it. "That's a candle. I had to light it because I think you're causing some problems with everything electrical in the vicinity of my life, right now. Do you want to see it close-up?" Josh leaned over to his left, picked up the vanilla-scented votive and brought it to the closer edge of the table, to Al's right, and the alien slowly moved toward it, all the while staring at the glowing yellow flame on top. Josh wondered if it could smell the vanilla in the air, like he could, and if so…how?? He saw no nostrils or orifices for smelling anywhere on Al, so maybe his skin itself had the sense of smell? Maybe its skin possessed other senses, who knew? It moved right up next to the candle, put its eyes up next to the flame, and then suddenly it shook violently and made the weirdest sound, like a cough mixed with a burp, while its mouth simultaneously blew out the flame. The light from the window was practically gone now, but with what little was left, Josh could see a stream of smoke rising from the burnt wick, and he sighed to himself, because he then remembered that he used the last match he had on that candle. Al chirped once then looked back up at Josh, who quietly and simply said, "God bless you." And then the two just sat there, in the dark, with an occasional chirp/growl echoing through the house.

TIME OF THE TRYKKOR

Strangely, it did not take him long to reach the spire of the building, although the sweat on McCray's face and hands (his whole body, really) would suggest an arduous and lengthy climb. As he crawled out through the hatch, and onto the roof's platform, he felt no wind, which again was surprising, since he was now over 500 feet above campus. He instinctively looked upward, and stared at the ominous, charcoal cloud cover that was miles above him, stretching far across the horizon...beyond the city, the hilltop neighborhoods, and the confluence of the three rivers. There was also an orange, fire-like hue that glowed and resonated between the clouds; he could feel a strange heat being suppressed on top of him, only adding to the copious beads of perspiration occupying his forehead. He was breathing heavy, and in the air he could sense a dense, thick odor of what he could only imagine dread smelled like. It enveloped the complete atmosphere that hovered over the Cathedral of Learning (or The Tower, as some call it)-the tall, iconic, gothic landmark building that resides at the center of the University of Pittsburgh.

He ran to the southern edge of the roof, peering over and down at the nearest balcony, which seemed to be about 100 feet or so below him. He could also see the lights of the vehicles on Forbes Avenue, as all were at a standstill and stretching for miles back towards downtown Pittsburgh. And for a brief moment, looking down Bigelow Avenue, where the old Forbes Field stadium stood decades ago, he couldn't help but think of the famous black and white George Silk photograph taken for Life Magazine, of the fans standing on the aforementioned perch on a sunny afternoon, watching the final game of the 1960 World Series between the Pirates and the Yankees. The outcome of that game would be more celebratory than this particular evening's forthcoming events, he feared.

He was sent to the roof to give support to Jasmyn, who was a type of quasi-religious soldier called a Sentinel, and he could see her down below, on the west side of the balcony. McCray looked around the roof, studying it for a few seconds, then looked back up to the skies, which had brought the arrival of what the Sentinel had referred to as the Trykkor: A demonic creation not seen for hundreds of years, that, as myth had it, was spawned out of Hell more than a millennia ago, in order to punish humanity for its sins before their souls were judged after death. The Sentinel is, in truth, an ancestor of the first humans to ever dispose of the Trykkor while the beast was in our world. Not many were privy to how its banishing took place, and through the centuries it had been accomplished more than once; one thing was known, though - when the Trykkor would appear again, it was a Sentinel who was always sought out and called upon to where the demon was thought to be entering into our world. Sentinels were descendants of ancient spiritual warriors, called *Augurs*, who possessed a clairvoyant ability to predict when and where the creature would appear. However, with the help of 21st Century technology, along with some contemporary wisdom, insight and instinct, Dr. Roger Mears' group of university grad students and his colleague, Professor Donald Heatherington, had discovered and predicted that tonight's visit would happen smack dab in the middle of campus.

As McCray looked down at the balcony, he watched as the Sentinel slowly made her way toward a large smoldering pile of rock, ember and ash that had, at first, shot out of a huge hole in the Earth - a crevice that had stretched across the courtyard that separated the Cathedral from Heinz Chapel, which stood 200 yards East of the towering structure. The mass had launched its way skyward, out of the bowels of the underground, up into the heavens with such speed that it broke the sound barrier with a thunderous crack that shattered countless windows throughout the Tower. It disappeared into the dark cloud cover miles above, then came streaking back down to Earth, landing firmly on top of the Indiana limestone surface of the Tower's 40th floor balcony.

McCray remembered Professor Heatherington's postulation that there was a strange, metaphysical bond between the chapel and the Cathedral. The chapel had been built soon after the Cathedral's completion, and for decades there was a secret belief among locals that a supernatural link existed between the two structures, beyond their similar gothic structures, and perhaps this link might hold a deeper purpose. No one could have guessed, however, that it would be to create a gateway between worlds, allowing a demonic creation to crossover, encased in a molten-like shell that was still billowing smoke, as McCray peered at it from above.

The actual landing spot was unexpected by both Jasmyn and the group. An earth-bound arrival and encounter had been theorized, but when the fiery bolus actually landed *on* the Tower, a makeshift Plan B had to be enacted. And this is where McCray found himself; he had weapons training through his experience in the school's ROTC program, and so was tasked to gain a position above the balcony in order to give "higher ground" support to the Sentinel while she calmly yet expeditiously assembled a device that was going to somehow capture the beast, supposedly keeping it imprisoned and immobile while she planned a way of using a unique supernatural element called *etheros*, which held the power to send the creature back to its hellish dominion. This was something he had been waiting to see, and now he had the best seat in the house for it.

Jasmyn kept her distance as she walked the balcony, trying to decide where the best place would be to begin constructing the device, with the process being pretty simplistic. Separated, it was pieces of arrow-like metal shards, a large circular clasp with hinges around its circumference, and a steel chain that had a length of 50 feet. When all the pieces were connected together, they achieved the appearance of a steel claw with a long, metal tether that she would anchor to the limestone balcony floor with large, iron bolts. She could feel a strong, euthermic pulse generating from the rock-encrusted capsule, and decided that planting the iron bolt between it and the doorway behind her, leading back into the building's immense and distinguished Babcock Room, would give her an escape route, in case things didn't go as planned. She had placed her bags of equipment down as soon as she stepped onto the balcony, and began to rummage through them, placing each particular piece of metal and chain before her in an organized grouping; she had done this before. Just like the military, who trained their soldiers to disassemble and reassemble their rifles, she had been taught how to construct her own weapon so well that she could do it in her sleep, or under water, or even in full-force hurricane gales. And she had to be that deft with it, because time was definitely a factor in this situation.

Inside the Tower, the group was frantically digging through the mountains of data and meta-analyses that the event had been generating from the various software models and computer programs. Lucy and another student, Jeff, were plowing through atmospheric and thermodynamic figures and computations, while Prof. Heatherington and Dr. Mears studied multiple readings derived from various strategically placed antenna-like devices, called 'sky wires', which had been planted throughout the façade of the building, as well as across the lawn and over to the grounds of the chapel. These were to assist in anticipating, hopefully, the moment of contact with the Trykkor. However, since they had not anticipated an actual landing on top of the Tower itself, the readings from the devices would need to be more efficiently scrutinized, with the ones left on the commons yard being practically useless now. But they felt they still had to try to find a somewhat accurate timeframe of when the creature would arise from its protective chrysalis.

Dr. Mears scanned through pages of data, and then looked over at Jeff. "What are you finding over there, Jeffrey?" "Hold on, I'm checking the Farmer's Almanac right now," the student replied. "This is no time for games!" Mears exclaimed. Jeff tittered as he replied, "We only put four antennas on that balcony, and there probably should be at least twice that many to get an accurate meas-" The doctor interrupted, "What do you have so far?!" "Barometric readings have dropped considerably in the past 10 minutes, and the—" Mears stopped him again. "Define 'considerably'." Lucy decided to join in the conversation. "It's dropped from 26.4 inHG to 25.83 inHG…and at this rate, it looks like it might even break 25." Professor Heatherington, listening the entire time while looking at a DOPPLER graph on his laptop, chimed in with a tone of gleeful disbelief. "That's impossible! The lowest ever recorded measurement was 25.17 during an F4 tornado. Those readings can't be correct – check them again."

Outside, on the roof, McCray could feel his ears popping, which temporarily distracted him from the scene on the balcony below. He felt a headache rapidly come on, while he noticed the warm feeling of liquid draining from his nose. He looked down to see a few droplets of blood on his shoes and the concrete roof, and put his arm up to wipe his nose and upper lip. As he wiped the blood away with his shirtsleeve, he wondered if the Sentinel was experiencing the same symptoms, or were they worse, due to her proximity to the thing?

On the balcony, things literally were heating up. She felt the temperature rising against her body, as she knelt down over her equipment. She attempted to stay calm and focused while she completed the assembly of the ensnaring device, but as the throbbing pulse of heat from the meteorite pummeled her, like a huge blow dryer being turned on and off, she could feel her heart rate rising and her breath becoming short and rapid. The rise in mercury was also causing the metal links of the trap to painfully warm up, as well, feeling like the iron handles of a boiling pot. She hoped her leather gloves would do the trick, but she knew there was only so much they could take before the tether would be untouchable. She continued to clasp together the final links to the entrapment, and hastened to finish its assembly, while fighting the enervating heat that cloaked the balcony, when the capsule began to vibrate and shake. In the meeting room, an alarm began to sound from one of the larger computers that Dr. Mears stood in front of. Heatherington ran over to his side, looking at the information that was flashing in red across the monitor, while Jeff and Lucy stood idle across the room, staring at the two gentlemen. "It's begun" was all that the doctor whispered.

Jasmyn heard a noise, as if an egg had been cracked open, and turned her attention to the orb. Seconds later, another crack. This one was louder than its predecessor. They seemed to be coming from the top of the mound, but she couldn't quite place specifically where. Then, she noticed a slight bulge occur at a point to her right, after which she spied what she believed to be the sharp, pointed tip of a horn penetrate through the orb's surface and protrude straight out and up into the air, and then it disappeared back down into the shell. A mist came shooting out of the hole it had left, giving off a snake-like hiss and having a sulfur-like aroma that was nauseating and burned her eyes and nostrils. She immediately reached into her duffle bag and took out a black breathing mask, which she slipped around her head and placed over her mouth and nose. This had an immediate effect on her respiratory system, allowing her to breathe comfortably, as she continued to work on the device. Again, another crack…and another. She looked at the orb, and could see multiple streams of mist, hissing out into the night air. She also noticed something different: There was not only one horn poking out, but two more appeared, and they seemed to be progressing with haste, now. The horns made holes that perforated the shell down its center, and she was just about finished with her task, when she felt a strong vibration come from the orb. With one last punch, the horns broke through to her far right, and tore back through all of the perforations they had just made, like a zipper unzipping itself. Clouds of steam billowed out as the two encrusted halves broke apart, and she watched as the beast emerged from the smoke and rubble.

It lifted its three-horned head out of the shell, and pushed the remnant halves off to its sides with two arms that were huge and muscular. The monster rose out of the remains and took a few deep breaths, then a couple of strides, slow and deliberate, forward onto the balcony tile. It was basked now in the Tower's floodlights that hung a number of floors above them. In this light, Jasmyn could see the demon in its entirety, as it stopped and stood fully upright, extending its arms and hands out over its head, bellowing with an incredible roar, announcing its presence to the world. Looking at it, Jasmyn thought it truly was as frightening a creature as one would expect coming out of Hell. She observed this: it stood about ten feet tall, had a humanoid figure, standing on two thick legs, with feet that were made up of three long toes on each foot, with each toe having a sharp, pointed nail at the end of it; its midsection and waist were smaller than its wide, hairy chest, and its arms were the size of its legs, with large hands that resembled those of a human's, with long, curled fingers that had the same razor-like nails that its feet possessed. Its shoulders were broad, and the neck was thick, which complimented the size of its chest, and its head was large in its own right, but was much less human than the rest of it. In fact, the head resembled more of a cross between a canine and a rhino, with one large horn that sat on top of its mouth and nose, and the two other horns were on top of its head, one over each eyebrow. There was no hair to be seen on its skull, which only made its yellow eyes standout that much more predominantly against the demon's ubiquitous rufescent skin.

Still frozen in sheer bewilderment, Jasmyn realized she had to act quickly; she didn't think the Trykkor was aware of her presence yet, so she continued her construction, ten yards away, being as quiet as possible as to not draw the least bit attention to herself. But, even as the thought crossed her mind, a piece of the metal chain fell from her hands, clanking down onto the balcony…and the Trykkor looked right at her. With a glance of menace and anger, it growled and seemed ready to pounce on her like a predator to its prey, when a bright spotlight hit it from above – a police helicopter was now hovering about three stories over the balcony, and the demon then gave the flying machine its full attention. Jasmyn thought that it must be the first time a Trykkor has seen anything like this before, because the beast seemed frozen in wonder and puzzlement…until gunfire began raining down from the chopper. However, the beast seemed impervious to the bullets, as they appeared to just ricochet off of its body and fall to the ground.

With its back to the Sentinel now, the Trykkor watched the helicopter as it slowly adjusted its aerial position, guns silent for the moment, which made Jasmyn think that the airborne sniper was reloading. The demon, giving off another loud low-end growl towards the chopper, then hunched over, arching its back, and that's when she saw them: out of two muscular humps on either side of the beast's back, came two protrusions that then enlarged and stretched out horizontally, to the left and right, until they each reached a span of about ten feet. The Trykkor's wings were venous, dark brown in color, and retained the muscular appearance that the rest of its anatomy shared. They were more bat-like than bird, and it began to flap them, slowly and fluidly, but with a force that moved and scattered the orb debris across the balcony tile, and Jasmyn could feel the warm air on her face as it blew her long, scarlet hair back off of her shoulders. She took an elastic band from around her wrist and tied her hair in a tail, wanting to avoid any opportunity for it to fall into her face and block her vision; she knew she couldn't afford to take her eyes off of her enemy for an instant.

After a couple of large, swift movements from its wings, the Trykkor launched itself upward, right at the chopper. Again, the floodlights illuminated everything, so she could see the beast ascend vertically, right to the height of the helicopter, and stop just short of the flying machine's whirling blades. Gunfire began to erupt again from inside the chopper, and this time the demon fought back. Its horns and torso began to turn a bright yellow-gold glow, then a burst of what looked to Jasmyn to be liquid fire came spewing from the beast's mouth, hitting the helicopter directly on its side, where the sniper was sitting and shooting from. The chopper became fully engulfed in fire and flame, then exploded in midair, and dropped like a fiery stone, crashing onto the concrete sidewalk below. Onlookers on the ground had to scatter in all directions. The street was lined with police cruisers, with a multitude of officers flanking the cars and watching the unfolding events, and who now began firing their drawn weapons up at the Trykkor.

Jasmyn could hear the shots begin, and saw bullets hit some of the Tower's windows above her, but she knew she wasn't in any danger of being shot herself. While the beast was preoccupied with the chopper, she had been able to complete the device's construction, and now that the police on the street held its attention, she made the best of the opportunity. As the Trykkor descended down towards its new enemies, it came to a height that was close enough for the Sentinel to attempt to entrap the demon. She took the open-ended snare, and like a lasso, began to twirl the chained, jawed link over her head, and at precisely the right moment, she let fly. The device flung threw the air and hit the Trykkor above its left ankle. Upon contact, the claw collapsed and locked into place, clasping its metal jaws together. The demon, upon feeling the metal hit its skin, howled with anger and looked down at the claw, and followed the tether over to where Jasmyn was standing, clasping the chain in her hands, with the end of it anchored into the limestone at her feet. The Trykkor then gave out a roar that was louder than anything it had let out before. It immediately flew back to the Tower, ascending as it did so, trying to break free of its entrapment, but the chain was firmly nailed into the balcony, and it stopped the beast abruptly in mid-flight. It tugged a number of times, but it could not break free of the claw's embrace. Jasmyn watched it struggle, and she tried to guess what its next move would be. The beast would either continue its attempts to free itself, or swoop down in her direction and attack her. As she mulled over her options, the Trykkor vomited its lava breath down onto the chain links, trying to melt the metal and break the connection. But the links held, so the Trykkor stopped trying to free itself after a minute, and looked directly at the Sentinel, snarling at her, and then swooped down toward the balcony.

Before it could reach her, however, more gunfire began to hail down on the Trykkor from above, hitting the beast in its back, head and horns. It stopped short of the balcony, turned and looked upward to see McCray, high above them on the upper ledge of the Tower, aiming his high-powered rifle at it, like a hunter in his elevated hide. During all of this, he found himself surprisingly calm and mentally prepared for what he was witnessing and what needed to be done. The police chopper had accomplished some of his work, preoccupying the beast while the Sentinel did her thing with the trap, but now his talents and assistance were needed, as anticipated, and he didn't hesitate to act.

The Trykkor's eyesight was keen, and it could easily make out McCray up on the roof, peering down at it through his scope. With a large flap of its wings, it ascended upwards, concentrating fully on his location, and flew toward him until the chain once again had no slack, and it stopped cold in midair flight. As McCray continued to fire round after round at it, accurately hitting the beast in its torso and legs, the Trykkor took one long, deep breath, and its chest and horns began to glow again, as it then exhaled a long stream of liquid fire up and directly at McCray's position. He was startled to see this through his scope, and immediately leapt back and rolled away from the ledge, out of the way of the oncoming stream, which covered the entire perch with fire, flame and a massive heat blast that knocked him back even further away from his aforementioned position.

To Jasmyn, the sight was breathtaking. Watching the beast hover 50 feet over head, and project its fire, on a line, right up at the exact spot where McCray had been, was awesome in the most literal sense. She was so engrossed that she almost neglected to react to the falling lava stream that began to crash down onto the balcony. She had to race into the covered confines of the Babcock Room, as everything outside lit up with flames and light. The impact was powerful enough to shake the room's large windows facing the balcony, and a few cracks in the glass developed as a result, reaching from the tops of the frames and stopping in the middle of the panes. Jasmyn was knocked off her feet, onto the floor, and she staggered trying to stand back up; she was sweating profusely, and the air in the room was now thick, heavy and hot, even through the breathing mask she was still wearing. She thought that this must be what's it like to be trapped in a house fire, only without the smoke inhalation. That was the curious thing: with all of the fire and flame, there was hardly any smoke. Hot mist and steam were omnipresent on the balcony, as if it had been turned into a spa, but there was none of the dark, life-threatening smoke that one might expect.

While she gathered her faculties inside, the Trykkor, no longer able to see McCray on the roof, briskly alighted itself back onto the balcony, standing there and gathering knowledge of where the Sentinel might have gone, and ignoring the cacophony from the streets below. It peered around the balcony, briefly, and then looked to its right, at the windows of the Babcock Room. With the room flooded in darkness inside, all the demon could see was its own menacing reflection staring back in the glass. Making eye contact with itself was an unfamiliar experience, as it snarled and growled before it spit another burst of streaming liquid, this time at the far end of the line of windows to its right, and continued in a direct line straight across to its left, instantly smashing every pane of glass it hit. While millions of pieces of glass flew in all directions, the beast threw its head up and let out something of a victorious roar. Inside, Jasmyn had run for shelter behind the room's immense fireplace, which sat against the wall perpendicular to the windows, and protected her from the devastation that had just been delivered. When it was over, she peered out from her hiding place, and saw the balcony's side of the room completely on fire, from the carpeted floor to the multiple pieces of furniture strewn about to the various pictures and paintings on the walls...and now black smoke began to fill the room.

McCray, meanwhile, could not stay on the roof anymore. His post had been destroyed, and there was nowhere to see the balcony, now. So, he crept back down the ladder and staircase and he decided that his best course of action was to make his way downstairs and try to locate the Sentinel. That was his task, to support her cause, no matter what the cost. Upon meeting her hours before, he had felt an immediate kinship with her, which he knew went beyond any physical attraction or desire; it was her soul's purpose that he understood and instantly bonded with. As much as she wanted to protect and defend humanity from the Trykkor, he wanted to protect *her from it*, and he rushed to get to her side and provide whatever assistance he could; he just hoped that by the time he found her, it wouldn't be too late.

Meanwhile, Dr. Mears, et al had given up on the data and computations, and decided that heading to the ground floor and going outside to witness the event for themselves on Fifth Ave., was the best thing for the group to do. Lucy and Jeff burst through the ground floor exit doorway first, followed by Heatherington and Mears. They ran down the sidewalk and all four, sprinting to be street side as quickly as possible, looked behind them, desiring to see what was occurring on the balcony. But the view was blocked by the north face of the Tower, so when they reached the street, they scurried down towards the Bigelow Ave. side of the Cathedral, through the sea of spectators lining the sidewalk. The wreckage of the helicopter was still on fire, in a heap directly in front of where they stopped, with the smell of fuel and burning metal filling the air, and the charred bodies of the chopper's crew in plain sight. From this vantage point, they could see the creature as it flew up and sprayed what looked like fire from its mouth, up toward the top of the Tower, at which time Jeff exclaimed, "Oh, shit! That's where Mac was supposed to be, I think!" The Trykkor then hastily flew back down to the balcony, pieces of flaming debris falling downward with it, as it landed out of sight.

The view from the ground was too far below and obstructed for anyone to see what the beast was doing on the balcony; all they could hear were the sounds of smashing glass and explosions as a sun-like hue encompassed the balcony. Between the cries and yelling of the terrified crowd, Jeff said, "Well...I think they were going to renovate the Babcock Room anyway." Without looking, Lucy swung her hand around and hit him on the shoulder. Shrieks and screams cried out from all around them, and some bystanders ran away from the crowd, only to have their spaces immediately filled by more curious and bewildered folk behind them. Lucy couldn't help but think that maybe they would have been safer inside the building. She could sense the mortal danger that both McCray and the Sentinel were in, and also felt a slight tinge of doubt that she herself would live to see the sun rise tomorrow morning. But her curiosity, like everyone else's, kept her firmly planted in her spot. Then Jeff said, "I can't help but feel extremely superfluous at this point." She looked at him, grabbed his hand, and turned to look at Dr. Mears and Professor Heatherington, who were awestruck, mouths gaping open, and the light show on top of the balcony reflecting off of their eyeglasses.

Inside the Babcock Room, the sprinkler system had gone off, dousing the fire that had engulfed the majority of the room. Jasmyn stayed put in her hidden, crouched position behind the fireplace, soaking wet and feeling more scared than before. Although she couldn't see it, she knew the Trykkor was still outside...she could feel its presence. She removed the air filter from around her face, then looked up at the ceiling, through the cold, spraying water, and guessed that it was no more than eight feet high, which meant that the demon might be too large to simply walk into the room from the outside, and made her think that maybe she was safe, for the time being. The Trykkor, in fact, was still slowly pacing back and forth on the balcony, stepping on broken glass and pieces of window frame, peering into the room. Jasmyn then noticed its shadow moving along the back wall that faced the balcony, so she knew it was just her in the room, which gave her pause. Then, after a moment, through the noise of the falling water, she heard a deep, baleful voice: "Sentinel! I know you're in there, cowering in fear; hiding will do you no good. I will soon be free of my chains, and then you will have no hope of surviving. For I am here, on this night, for you, Sentinel! My master has tasked me to remit *your* soul into his possession." Its voice sent shivers down her spine, and she came to the instant realization that she might actually be screwed, here. And as that thought sprinted through her mind, the sprinkler system shut off, and her aquatic security blanket was now just a collection of puddles in the saturated carpeting. She soon found, however, that her instinct was correct; after its speech, the demon tried to enter the room, but was too large to simply walk right in, and had to crouch down to such a degree that, after only a few steps, it found itself wedged between the floor and the ceiling, like trying to fit a circle into the space of a square. Jasmyn, looking carefully around the corner of the fireplace, could see it struggling to maneuver into the room, and took note of its mistake. The Trykkor attempted to enter sideways, and had turned its back to the far wall, where the fireplace and Jasmyn were. Now, stuck with its back to her, it had no line of sight, and she immediately decided to make a clandestine move to exit.

She snuck out of her hiding place, and like a cat creeping by a sleeping dog, slowly stepped passed the fireplace, against the wall and toward the balcony, trying to keep the squishing of her steps into the water-logged floor as quiet as possible. She could feel her leather boots sink into the carpet step by saturated step, as she finally came to the shattered window frame, with its chards of glass covering the entire area leading outside and which would be unavoidable to walk on in order to exit the room. She took a couple of light cautious steps onto the debris, but her weight snapped and crunched the pieces of glass under her feet, and she glanced over at the Trykkor, who, still struggling to get into the room, quickly looked back to the wall behind it. Seeing the Sentinel standing there, it roared and instinctively tried to move towards her, which caused it to become even more tightly wedged inside the room. Jasmyn reacted by bursting through the window frame and ran nimbly over to her weapons bag, which had been relocated to the far right balcony corner, just passed the Trykkor.

As she broke for the bag, the beast had tried to spray her with its fire, but she had moved too quickly, and all it hit was the side of the wall, which erupted into flames behind her. As she reached the ledge, the beast turned its head back around to face the outside, and could see her position on the balcony directly, now. She knew this, but decided that this might be her only chance at defeating it, while it was immobilized inside the room. As it caught sight of her, hastily digging through her black bag, it hissed out an exclamation: "I have you, Sentinel! You have no place to hide, now!" Jasmyn heard it take a long, deep breath, and found herself frozen with fear. She had not found the etheros yet, and now her time was up. She felt a survival instinct react, and tried to take a quick step back toward the other side of the balcony, but slipped on the rocky debris covering the tile floor, falling onto her hands and knees, as she looked up to see the Trykkor preparing to spit its deadly fire at her.

At that moment, McCray crashed through the interior door of the Babcock Room, rifle at the ready, and without hesitation, began shooting at the demon just as it was about to strike Jasmyn. The beast could feel the sharp impact of the bullets pummeling the back of its head, and it turned back in anger to see him, twelve feet away, yelling "Go back to Hell!" As he stood there, firing his gun in heroic fashion, the Trykkor stretched out its right wing, long into the room and knocking McCray off his feet, back against the far wall. His rifle dropped to floor, back to his left, and though he was stunned, he sat up, reached over, grabbed the gun and took aim at the monster, but not before it had sent its liquid fire streaming over to him. McCray had no time to react, as he was engulfed entirely in the furious onslaught, and then he was gone.

The Trykkor stared at its accomplishment for a moment then turned its head to the balcony, but the Sentinel was no longer next to the ledge. The beast then used all of its might to push and heave itself through the back out of the room, falling onto the balcony floor as chunks of wall and ceiling flew off in all directions, then stood upright, shaking off the pieces of Tower and Babcock Room that had hitch-hiked all over its body and wings. It gathered itself, broadening its ominous airfoils to their full wingspan, as it curiously walked over to the ledge and looked down to the crowd below. Everything seemed puny and weak to it from here, and it used its wings to raise itself off of the balcony.

Lucy, still clenching Jeff's sweaty hand with hers and staring up at the Tower, leaned over to him and asked, "How did she say she was going to kill it?" "She can't really kill it," Jeff answered. "It's a supernatural being, and she explained that the only power she has is to use something she called 'etheros', which is a compound powder of sorts; a substance that, when used against the Trykkor, negates its existence on Earth and banishes its spirit back to hell." "How is she going to use it??" she responded. Jeff paused a second, then said "I think she told us it has to breath the stuff in. The demon has to take it into its body, and then it acts as a philter against the Trykkor's soul. I tried to follow her explanation as close as I could, but I'm still kinda lost on how any of this has been remotely possible."

The chain became taut almost immediately, as the Trykkor elevated its position above the balcony. It seemed to be momentarily fixated on all of the lights and noises coming from the streets beneath it, as well as the increasing number of helicopters that had arrived farther overhead, failing to take heed of the violent, deadly conclusion of their predecessor. These were news choppers now, shining spotlights down upon the beast, illuminating the balcony and side of the building, so that the Trykkor's exaggerated shadow was cast upon the side of the Cathedral, making an even more threatening sight. The beast looked around its surroundings again, catching a glimpse of Heinz Chapel and the crevasse between the church and the Cathedral. This sight made the beast snicker - almost chuckle to itself - as it hovered in the one spot for a moment, then let out a long exhale before it took a deep breath and shot its liquid fire straight across Bigelow Blvd., and directly into the tree line that ran parallel to the Tower's grounds. Like a giant flamethrower, it sprayed the foliage across the street, moving its head left to right, painting the trees with a burning orange and red arc, and when it was finished, the entire street was a light from the fire that had engulfed the tops of the trees. Burning leaves, limbs and branches, along with scattered streams of liquid fire, were falling to the street and sidewalk below, where the area was so saturated with students and pedestrian on-lookers, that they could not escape the fiery onslaught of lava and debris. Bodies seemed to melt as they were hit by the falling lava, some bursting into flames from head to toe, while vehicles exploded upon contact. Up the street, at the intersection, Mears and his group stood there in terror and wonder, as did the rest of the crowd, fearing what would happen next. Lucy looked over at Professor

Heatherington, who was biting his fingernails feverishly, and she found herself momentarily distracted by this; the nerves and anxiety were a side of the professor that she had never seen in the four years she had known him.

The Trykkor turned to look at the chain, which was still binding it to the balcony floor, and saw that lying next to the base of it, was the Sentinel. She was face down among the scattered debris, partially buried and covered with dust, dirt and various parts of the Babcock Room. A small stream of orange saliva fell from the demon's mouth, landing just a few inches away from Jasmyn's face, and it slowly descended down toward her, landing just to the side of where she had fallen, as it observed her motionless body for a moment. It then reached down with its massive hand, and turned her over on her back, noticing streaks of blood on her face and neck. The beast let out a low, disapproving growl, and preceded to pick her up and brought her limp body closer to its face, for a more intimate inspection of her condition; her arms and legs just dangled in the air, appearing like a dirty old rag doll that had been found in the trash. It made a couple of sniffs with its long snout of a nose, growled again, more intensely this time, and squeezed her body a bit more tightly as it then let out a long exhale, then began to take a deep breath. That was when the Sentinel's eyes opened and her two hands came clashing together, causing a plume of powder to erupt from the collision, directly into the Trykkor's face. She had been holding the etheros in her fists, and now the beast had snorted it directly into its upper respiratory tract. It threw its head up and back, making an ear-piercing screech, and dropped her from its grasp. It had carried her back into the air, and when she dropped, they weren't over the balcony anymore, but had floated out over the ledge, and she barely caught the side of it as she fell. The leather gloves she had been wearing allowed her to grip the rough corner of the ledge and catch her falling weight, but now she was in the most vulnerable position possible, as the demon ferociously crashed to the balcony surface, still roaring at the top of its infected lungs. It struggled to find where she had landed, frantically looking around the balcony, kicking and pushing anything and everything out of its way, either off the ledge or back into the charred remains of the Babcock Room, then spied her hands clinging to the ledge, and yelled to her, "I will not be defeated, Sentinel! You are mine for the taking, and your soul will burn for all eternity!" And with that, the Trykkor took one last deep, heavy breath, and heaved its fiery breath at her. However, nothing came out of it this time, and the monster began choking and gagging, as its orange and red hue turned to a pale white, and it fell to its knees, grasping its throat with both immense hands. Its breaths became shorter and shorter, and it began to violently flap its wings, but to no avail; it could not gain the strength to do anything, and simply collapsed to the floor. It attempted to lift its body up one last time, but gave in to the weakness brought on by the etheros, and finally, in a bright explosion of white light that enveloped the Trykkor's entire body, it was gone, leaving only a trail of glowing points of light in its place, like curious fireflies that headed off into the night sky.

Bathed in light from the helicopters, the balcony was empty and still. On the ledge, Jasmyn was finally able to gather the strength to lift herself up and over the balcony's side and back onto the floor, landing on her back, completely out of breath. She stared up into the lights that hovered overhead, and after a few cautious moments of gathering her faculties together, she lifted herself up and took in what was left in front her. It looked like the Babcock Room had exploded, leaving the destructive results lying all over the balcony, as well as the remains of the orb that had not been thrown to the ground. That was it. No sign of the Trykkor save for a faint outline of its shape that could be seen on the tile floor, with the claw and chain encircling it. She again looked skyward, past the helicopters and lights, and saw that the dark clouds that had preceded the demon's arrival were now dispersing themselves across the region, while a welcomed breeze began to blow around the building. As the zephyr surrounded her, Jasmyn closed her eyes, took a deep breath of the crisp, clean, cool air and, with a thought of gratitude to McCray, slowly and triumphantly exhaled…

ABOUT THE AUTHOR

J. David Hanlin, Jr. was born and raised in Pittsburgh, PA, and is a proud graduate of the University of Pittsburgh. He lives in Los Angeles.